NOT SO SHY

NOA NIMRODI

KAR-BEN
PUBLISHING

KAR-BEN PUBLISHING®
An imprint of Lerner Publishing Group, Inc.
241 First Avenue North
Minneapolis, MN 55401 USA

Website address: www.karben.com

Cover illustration by Miriam Serafin.

Main body text set in Bembo Std.
Typeface provided by Monotype Typography.

Library of Congress Cataloging-in-Publication Data

Names: Nimrodi, Noa, 1969– author.
Title: Not so shy / by Noa Nimrodi.
Description: Minneapolis, MN : Kar-Ben Publishing, [2023] | Audience: Ages 9–14. | Audience: Grades 4–6. | Summary: Twelve-year-old Shai hates having to move to America and is determined to find a way to get back home to Israel—until she starts opening up to new experiences and friendships.
Identifiers: LCCN 2022010032 (print) | LCCN 2022010033 (ebook) | ISBN 9781728427911 | ISBN 9781728427928 (paperback) | ISBN 9781728481128 (ebook)
Subjects: CYAC: Immigrants—Fiction. | Jews—United States—Fiction. | Friendship—Fiction. | Middle schools—Fiction. | Schools—Fiction. | LCGFT: Novels.
Classification: LCC PZ7.1.N57 No 2023 (print) | LCC PZ7.1.N57 (ebook) | DDC [E]—dc23

LC record available at https://lccn.loc.gov/2022010032
LC ebook record available at https://lccn.loc.gov/2022010033

Manufactured in the United States of America
1-49348-49453-8/29/2022

I dedicate this book to all those who
call more than one place home.

And in memory of Rachel Nimrodi,
my mother-in-law and second mom,
who always focused on the good.
You are in my heart forever.

CHAPTER 1

NOSES, DISASTERS, AND SNICKERDOODLES

Ema bangs another nail into the wall with her pink sparkly hammer. She's excited that it's easier to hang things here since the houses are made of wood, not bricks. Both my parents think everything is easier here in America.

Bam!

I can't stand the pounding and the echoing through the half-empty house, and I can't stand the ceramic heart she just put up that says, "Home is where the heart is." My heart is twelve thousand kilometers away.

I wish she would cool it down with that hammer— I can't concentrate. I need to concentrate. Planning how to kill your father's boss is a serious matter.

I grab my sketchbook, stomping my feet hard as I walk past Ema so she'll know I'm annoyed with her banging. But the ugly beige carpet swallows the sound effect and ruins the drama.

I sit in the backyard on one of the new lounge chairs. Why is the grass fake? Green is a hard color to imitate. The weather feels fake too, like somehow an air conditioner has been installed in the sky. How can it be so cool in August?

I browse through my sketchbook—it's mostly butterflies. Butterflies are my specialty. My favorite thing about them is that they don't have noses. I mean, I'm pretty good at drawing almost anything, except noses.

I've researched possible natural disasters in San Diego. Earthquakes. Fires. Tsunamis. I draw Abba's boss buried under rubble. Next, I draw him caught up in flames. Good job avoiding the nose. He doesn't deserve to have a nose anyway. It's all his fault that we're here now.

Motek runs outside and jumps into the swimming pool. A week ago, when we left Israel, he was taken in a big cage, the Lab half of him crying, the Dalmatian half barking like crazy. He knew even less than we did about where we were headed. Now he thinks he's a dolphin. I watch him swimming laps.

What's the use of having a pool at home if you don't have friends to invite over? Making friends was never a problem for me, but what if nobody understands my accent here? Maybe I won't talk. But how do you make friends without talking?

Motek climbs up next to me and shakes off the water from the pool, causing the orange flames on my drawing to spread. I'm such a horrible person. Abba's boss must have children who love him as much as we loved

Abba before he made us move here. Why did he have to hire Abba? Couldn't he find some molecular biologist in America to develop non-browning avocados?

I go over the fire flames with a blue marker, turning them into butterfly wings. Motek shakes off next to me again. Now the blue butterflies are smeared all over the page.

"*Die*, Motek!" I yell.

"Ahemmm . . ."

I turn around. A girl about my age is standing next to our fence. Silky skin, long black hair almost as long as mine but perfectly straight. She's dressed as if she's just gotten off the stage of some quirky musical. Striped colorful socks pulled up to her knees, red skirt with white polka dots. Kind of cool, but not the type of cool that *cool* kids would consider cool. She's holding a plate of cookies in her hands. Her purple bra strap is showing. Of course, she's wearing a bra, like most girls my age. It's just me that's flat as pita bread.

"Hi," she says, adjusting her bra strap. Oops. I guess I was staring.

Motek barks at her. I should open the gate and let her in, but I'm afraid Motek will run out and never come back. I wouldn't blame him.

"Die, Motek!" I yell again.

The striped-socks girl stares hard at me. "You're telling your dog to die?"

"Oh—no." I feel my face growing redder than her skirt. "*Die* means 'enough' in Hebrew."

"Oh." A smile spreads across her face. "A Hebrew-speaking dog. That's awesome. You all just moved here, right? I'm Kay-Lee."

"I'm Shai," I answer, aware right away that it sounds like I'm saying that I'm shy.

"It's okay, I'm used to shy people. My sister is also shy. What's your name?"

"Shai is my name. And I'm not actually shy." This is going to be tough. My name has the wrong meaning here, and on top of that, I realized at the airport that the right spelling is causing the wrong pronunciation—the guy checking our passports called me Shay, so I'm guessing I'll have to correct every teacher at roll call.

"Oh, sorry. Cool name."

"Thanks," I say, hoping my *th* sounds okay. Sticking your tongue between your teeth is not a sound that exists in Hebrew.

"Is it short for Shyleen?" Kay-Lee asks.

"No." Ugh. "It's not short for anything."

She pulls the cookie plate closer to her body and shifts her weight from one foot to the other. I've made her uncomfortable, and it makes me uncomfortable too. I was never like that in Israel, not even with people I'd just met. I hold on to Motek's collar and open the gate for Kay-Lee.

"Shai means *gift* in Hebrew," I say. I better get used to having to explain my name. I don't tell her the story of being born on Rosh Hashanah and how my parents decided that I was their gift for the new year. I'm afraid I'll mess up the whole story in English. Too bad you can't cover up accents with butterflies.

"My sister and I made some snickerdoodles for you and your family," Kay-Lee says.

Did she call the cookies sneaker-poodles? English is weird.

She points up to the window of their house. "That's my sister, Zoe."

I look up. Kay-Lee's little sister looks like Dora the Explorer. Gili is going to love this girl. I wave to her. She half smiles and backs up a little. But I can see she's still there, looking at me.

Motek is barking at Kay-Lee. She's holding tight to the cookie plate.

"Why is Motek barking like that?" Ema comes outside, followed by Gili. That's when she notices Kay-Lee.

"Welcome to the neighborhood," Kay-Lee says to my mom, handing her the cookie plate. "My sister and I baked these cookies for you. They're gluten free and non-GMO."

Gili and I look at each other. My English is better than hers, but I don't understand any more than she does what Kay-Lee just said about those poodle cookies.

"Tank you," Ema says. Oh gosh, her accent is worse than mine.

Kay-Lee introduces herself.

"I'm Gili!" my sister volunteers.

"Hi, Gill-ee," says Kay-Lee, echoing the hard G.

"I would love to meet your parents," Ema says.

Kay-Lee's smile shrinks. Her mouth is now as tiny as the polka dots on her skirt. "It's just me and Zoe and my dad now," she says. "And my grandma." She bends down and pulls her socks above the knees. Her polka dot mouth opens just a little and closes, like she can't decide what to say next. "Well, I have to go now," she finally says, straightening her skirt. "See you."

"Thanks. For. OMG-cookies," Gili yells after her. She almost sounds American already.

"You're welcome." Kay-Lee turns around and laughs, like the whole embarrassing no-mom situation never happened.

CHAPTER 2

BRIBES, UGLY BEIGE CARPET, AND A BROKEN HEART

Abba comes home with bribes. He says they're gifts, but I know he's just bribing us to like America.

First, he kisses Ema and compliments her on the perfect spot where she hung the ceramic heart. Then he hands me a pack of acrylics—forty-eight colors. And brushes. The expensive type. And he kisses the top of my head. I give him a quick thank-you hug—not the type I would normally give for getting something I love. And I don't smile either. I vowed to never smile after we moved to America, though I'm not sure how long I can last. I'm not the miserable type.

"What did you get me?" Gili jumps on Abba.

"I thought you'd never ask. Come check this out." Abba lifts her up and carries her to the garage.

Gili comes back in with a boogie board taller than she is. It has an image of Dora the Explorer printed on it. "Yay!" She dances all around the house hugging it.

Way too happy. I should have given her a briefing on acting miserable in America.

"Did you see that our neighbor looks like Dora?" I ask Gili.

"The OMG-cookies girl? No, she doesn't," Gili says.

"Not Kay-Lee, her sister. She seems about your age, and she looks exactly like Dora. For real."

"Can I go see?" Gili looks at Ema. "Please."

Ema has the sparkly pink hammer in her hand again, planning what to hang next. "We'll invite them over once we're settled in," she answers.

"I wanna see her now," Gili says.

"She's not an exhibit," I tell Gili. "But actually, she was standing next to the window before. Let's go check. Maybe she's still there." I run upstairs. Gili follows me, pulling the boogie board that keeps sliding out from under her armpit.

I go into Gili's room, straight to the window that faces the neighbors' house. "Dora's not there anymore," I say.

Gili's right behind me, holding the boogie board on her head now. She looks disappointed.

"Hey." I have an idea that will take her mind off Dora the neighbor. "Give me that boogie board for a second."

"It's mine," she says. Such a six-year-old.

"I know it's yours," I say, "but the genius idea of how to have fun with it inside the house is mine. So you want to hear it?"

Gili twists her finger around her pigtail like she always does when she's seriously considering something.

"We can put this ugly carpet to use," I say. "Give it to me."

She hands it over.

I set the board at the top of the stairs and sit on it. "Stand behind me and give me a push."

Gili's finger is working that pigtail full speed.

"Come on," I say, "you can go right after me. It's going to be fun."

She pushes.

I fly down the stairs. "Yippee!"

Gili squeals.

"Whaaaaaaa!"

No! The boogie board goes flying out from under me in the direction of the ceramic heart on the wall. I hear it before I see it: Ema's gift from her sister is in pieces all over the floor.

"Ouch!" I land at the bottom of the stairs. I can't get up. My arm is bent at an angle that it's not supposed to be. I'm going to faint from the pain. Ceramic bits are scattered all around.

"My boogie board!" Gili yells.

Ema and Abba come running.

"Did you break anything?" Abba asks, leaning to check on me.

I lift my head slowly. "I can't move my arm," I say

and look at Ema. "I'm sorry I broke your heart."

"It's okay," Ema says. But her upper teeth are biting her lower lip, and that's always a sign that she's upset. Gili checks that her boogie board isn't broken.

"I'll get you some ice." Ema gets all practical but keeps talking all the way to the kitchen. "Try not to move, Shai. I think you broke it. Oy vey! Just what you need right before school starts, poor thing." She's back with a bag of ice. "What's gotten into you anyway? Riding down the stairs on a boogie board? And dragging Gili with you on this dangerous adventure—what were you thinking?" she scolds me while freezing my arm, not expecting an answer, I hope. She turns to Gili. "Go put your shoes on."

"Where are we going?" Gili asks.

Abba helps me up. "I'm taking Shai to see a doctor," he says.

"And I'm coming too?" Gili jumps up and down as if he said we're going to Disneyland. She runs upstairs and comes right back down, shoes in her hand.

"Gili, you're staying with me. Shoes, please, so you won't step on ceramic pieces and hurt yourself."

As soon as we get in the car, Abba makes a call. A lady gives him an address of an orthopedist's office.

"That was the relocation specialist they assigned to me at work," Abba says, answering a question I didn't ask. So they have specialists here to support people who ruin their children's lives? That's my question, but I don't ask.

He takes out a piece of gum from the glove compartment. I can smell the mint as he unwraps it. He folds the gum into two uneven parts and shoves it into his mouth. He offers me a piece. He used to remember I hate mint.

"I know it's not just your arm," Abba says as he backs the car out of the driveway. "I know it's hard for you."

I glue my forehead to the window and swallow hard. My arm hurts too much for me to have this conversation right now.

"It will get easier. I promise."

How can he promise? He only thinks of himself, his career. How can he be so selfish? Move an entire family across the world for his non-browning avocados.

"Why can't you just let things stay the way they are?" I yell, without meaning to. "Avocados are meant to brown. Why do you have to mess with nature?"

"Humans have always messed with nature, mostly in order to make our lives better. It's called progress. Change is scary, but . . ." He hits the brake a little too hard.

"Ouch!" The seatbelt cuts into my injured arm.

"Sorry. The yellow light doesn't blink here before it turns to red, like it does in Israel. I guess I'll have to get used to it."

While we wait for the green light, he looks at me. He strokes my cheek. "Sorry," he says again. He's apologizing about the sudden brake, not about moving here and making too many changes for all of us. The light turns green. "The clinic is right around the corner," Abba says. "Let's continue our discussion later. I want you to understand."

I shrug. He's the one who doesn't understand. It's obvious he'd rather have *me* rot than his beloved avocados.

CHAPTER 3

DR. HORSE, THE LORAX, AND A LIGHT BLUE CAST

The clinic looks new and clean, as if it was built this morning.
Abba fills out forms, and we wait to be called in.
Pictures from Dr. Seuss's books cover the walls. I loved
Dr. Seuss when I was little. I used to think he was
a horse doctor, since *seuss* means "horse" in Hebrew.
I remember the first time I read *The Cat in the Hat* in
English and realized it rhymes in English just as per-
fectly as it does in Hebrew. I bet his books rhyme in
other languages too.

I stare at a picture from *Oh, the Places You'll Go!*
The pain in my arm works its way to my stomach.
I wish I brought my sketchbook. I would make my
own version: *Oh, No! The Places I Don't Want to Go.*

A nurse with a pink outfit and a pink smile calls us
in. Gili would love her. She checks my temperature—
what does that have to do with me breaking my arm?
I don't ask. "Ninety-eight. Good," she says.

That's good?

Oh, it's Fahrenheit. If it was Celsius, I'd be soup.

She checks my weight and height, calling out numbers that sound completely wrong. It's not kilos and meters for sure. Numbers were supposed to be easy— the same—but they're losing their meaning here. Oof.

"The doctor will be in to see you shortly," the nurse says and leaves us to wait in the Cat-in-the-Hat room.

The doctor walks in. He's bald with fuzzy ginger eyebrows and a matching mustache. He looks like the Lorax, blending right in with the rest of the Seuss-themed office. First Dora the neighbor, now Lorax the doctor. Maybe it's my mind's way of trying to amuse me.

"I'm Dr. Lording." The doctor shakes Abba's hand and mine too. My left hand. The Lorax is excited to hear we're from Israel. "I traveled to Israel years ago," he says. "Best hummus in the world."

"Israel today might be different than you remember," Abba says, "but the hummus is still the best in the world."

"I must go again," the Lorax says, his eyebrows dancing like a pair of ginger caterpillars craving hummus.

I wish he'd stop talking about hummus and start examining my arm.

"So, right arm, but I see on the forms you're a lefty. So you did have a little bit of luck."

He's right about that. I'd die if I couldn't draw.

The Lorax moves my arm gently, but it still hurts. "Let's take an X-ray," he says. "You are most likely going to need a cast."

Cast? Like actors in a play? Am I auditioning for the lead role in this nightmare?

I look at Abba. He explains it to me in Hebrew. So my arm is probably broken, and my English is definitely worse than I thought.

* * *

The X-ray confirms a broken arm. They let me choose a color for my cast, which is pretty cool. I choose light blue.

"Matches your eyes," the pink nurse says.

My eyes are usually a very light blue, but if I wear green, they look green. Abba's eyes are the same. Ema and Gili have the type of blue that's always blue, no matter what they wear.

The cast goes all the way from my hand to my armpit.

"All done," says the nurse. "Now you can get all your friends to sign it."

I feel the tears coming. I never was good at controlling tears.

I imagine Ella, Tal, and Shir signing my cast. I can't even call and tell them I broke my arm because it's nighttime in Israel right now.

The Lorax hands me a tissue. "You can take Advil, up to four times a day," he says.

I don't know what Advil is, but I'm sure it's not something that can take away the pain of not having friends to sign my cast.

* * *

"That was quick and efficient," Abba says when we walk out of the clinic.

"Do you have to admire everything in America? I hate it here!" I don't care that I say it kind of loudly. Nobody understands Hebrew around here anyway.

"Lots to admire about America," someone behind us says. In Hebrew.

Abba and I both turn our heads. Right behind us are a tall, skinny red-haired woman and a short, balding man.

"Nice to hear Hebrew around here," says the man and introduces himself as Avi Levi. His wife, Lily Levi, squeaks, "Are you new here? Broken arm? Oh dear, oy vey. How did that happen?"

"Long story. And yes, we moved from Israel a week ago," Abba says. "Do you live around here?"

"About a thirty-minute drive. We come here for the international market. You should check it out. It has a lot of Israeli products." She points to a huge store right next to Dr. Lorax's office.

I look down into their cart and see a bag of couscous. Ema should know about this place.

Avi Levi tells Abba about his computer-support business, which he's had since they came here seventeen years ago. He says he's never going back to live in Israel, which he calls a lousy imitation of America. When he says that, Lily Levi's face crumples like she's about to sneeze, but she doesn't.

"We'd love to have you over for Shabbat dinner," she says. She pulls out the receipt from her shopping cart, scribbles a phone number, and hands it to Abba. "Have your wife call me." After that, she goes on and on about her daughter, who's apparently my age. Finally, Abba says we need to get back home and it was nice meeting them.

* * *

"I thought there were no Israelis around here," Abba says in the car. "Ema will be happy, don't you think?"

"I don't like the way he talked about Israel," I say. Abba doesn't answer.

I follow the Levis with my gaze. I see that Avi Levi just leaves the cart next to their car.

In Israel you can't do that. The shopping carts are all connected by chains, and you have to put a five-shekel coin in a slot on the cart to release it. The coin pops back out only when you return the cart to its place. Here, the stores trust people to return their carts, and people do. I actually like that about America. Avi Levi takes advantage of the trust system. I don't like him.

CHAPTER 4

SHABBAT SHALOM, FAIRY GODMOTHER, AND BAND

"Shai?" Ema's voice sounds far away, but as I open my eyes I see her next to me, sitting on the edge of my bed.

"Ready for the meeting with the school counselor?"

"Oof." As I lift my arm to my chest, I'm reminded of yesterday's stair surfing.

"You can take a pill before we leave," Ema says. There goes my excuse. "But not on an empty stomach. Come downstairs and have breakfast first. Do you need help getting dressed?"

"No," I say, even though I probably do. I slept in one of Abba's T-shirts since I couldn't get my pajamas on with the cast. He gave me his "Life Is Good" T-shirt, which I always loved. Now I hate it. I need a "Life WAS Good" one. I manage to wiggle myself into a loose tank top. I'm sweating by the time I'm done wrestling my favorite jeans on.

The only sounds I hear as I walk downstairs are my gurgling stomach and the ticking clock Ema hung in the hallway.

A row of cereal boxes is lined up on the kitchen counter. I pick one up. Froot Loops. The colors are so fake. Yuck. And I'm pretty sure the spelling is wrong. Actually, it's probably on purpose since the colors look nothing like real fruit.

"They don't cost that much here," Ema says. "I let Gili choose. I got waffles too. There are so many breakfast options in the frozen section, you wouldn't believe it." I hate that she sounds so excited—is she trying to prove that America is better than Israel?

"Where's Gili?" I ask.

"Abba took her to work with him so we can go see the counselor, just the two of us."

Ema sounds like it's some mother-daughter bonding activity. I wish Gili would have come with us—her cuteness could distract the counselor from miserable me.

The fake-fruit cereal colors the milk and looks disgusting, so I just take the pill without finishing the cereal. The idea of this school visit is making my stomach flip anyway; the medicine on an empty stomach is not going to make much of a difference.

"Let's call Saba and Safta and say 'Shabbat Shalom' before we leave," Ema says. New routine, I guess—instead of going to my grandparents' for Friday night dinner, we'll call them. It's morning here, but back home it's evening already. Friday dinner is like a holiday. Every week.

We FaceTime Safta. I see all my cousins running around at my grandparents' house, and I want to be there with them. "Shabbat Shalom!" they all yell, and Safta shows us the table.

White tablecloth, candles, a wine bottle next to Saba's plate. I want to shout, "Wait, I'm coming!" I want to scream that I'll find a way to come back. I don't care about Abba's avocados.

Ema tells Saba and Safta that we're going to visit my new school. I make sure my broken arm isn't showing on the video call. I don't want Safta to worry.

"Good luck, binti," Safta says. I love it when she calls me *binti*. It's Arabic, which is Safta's first language. It's like saying "my darling" or "my love" but it really means "my daughter." Even though she calls all her granddaughters that, it feels like she pronounces it in a special way when she says it to me.

"Shabbat Shalom," I say, my heart shrinking in my chest. "Bye." I do my best to sound cheerful for Safta. I'm not sure it's working.

"Bye!" Safta waves, and the reception goes bad. She blows pixilated kisses in the air. "See you in two weeks."

I look at Ema. "They're coming in two weeks? How come I didn't know that?"

"Because it was supposed to be a surprise, and your grandma just ruined it." Ema looks like someone just threw sand in her face.

Saba and Safta will be here in two weeks. I will convince them to take me back with them.

"I'll make us a nice Shabbat dinner tonight," Ema says. It was hard for her too, seeing them all together. Maybe this is my chance to point out that it was a mistake to move here and convince Ema we should go back.

My mouth locks down. In my head, I'm having this conversation with her, but she answers that we should be proud of Abba and support his career. "Urgh," I blurt out.

"You'll see." Ema says, "I'll make challah too."

* * *

We wait for the counselor to come in. Compared to my school back home, this school is newer, cleaner, brighter, bigger. My school in Israel could probably fit in this one four times. It looks like the schools I've seen in the movies and on TV. Well, figures—they're all filmed in America. I'm living in a movie.

Kids' art is up on the walls, same as in my school, but somehow it looks fancier. Maybe it's the textured walls or the framing. Soon my work will be up on these walls. My English might not be perfect, but that won't matter in art class.

I get my artistic talent from Ema—she's a jewelry designer—and my aunt Sigal, who is a ceramic artist.

"An improved variety of apples fell off *this* tree," Ema always says.

Of all her Ema Quotes that she repeats over and over, this is the least annoying one.

Ema had her own business back in Israel and was famous for her over-glittery style. I don't like glittery, but I'll admit she's creative. The only piece of jewelry I ever wear is the golden Star of David that Safta gave me for my bat mitzvah. Her grandmother gave it to her on her bat mitzvah, and when I turned twelve, she took it off her neck and put it around mine. It's a family heirloom that always skips a generation, passing from grandmother to granddaughter. Safta says it was made by a jeweler in Iraq a long time ago. I shift the star on the chain from side to side. Ema gives me her *don't-do-that* look. She's worried I'll break it. And maybe she's just a tiny bit jealous that it skipped her.

* * *

"Sorry to keep you waiting." The counselor floats into the room out of nowhere. She looks like the little fairy godmother from Cinderella and speaks in a matching soft fairy voice. I wish she could turn me into a pumpkin. That would make my life so much easier.

She asks about my broken arm, and Ema tells her the whole story in her broken English.

"Will you be able to take a couple of tests for me?" Ms. Fairy asks, looking at my arm.

"I'm left-handed," I say. I kind of wish I was right-handed at this moment.

She smiles her fairyland smile again. "You both have beautiful eyes," she says.

I wonder why people are more impressed with our eyes here. Her eyes are blue and pretty too, but not as big as ours. Maybe Americans are just more into giving compliments.

"The thick, long eyelashes she gets from her dad," Ema says. "Both my kids have them."

Oh boy. Here it comes: her worst but her personal-favorite Ema Quote: "I need a lot of mascara to compete with the rest of the family." She never gets sick of saying that. The Fairy fakes a polite giggle.

"All right, Shai, we'll just have you take two short assessment tests—one in English and one in math. After that, you can join your mom and me back here in my office. Okay, dear?"

I nod. Do I have a choice?

She leads me to a different room and leaves me alone to take the tests. The smell of her fairy-dust perfume stays in the room with me.

I take the English test first, and I feel stupid. Really stupid. The air conditioning is on full blast. I'm freezing.

When I start to take the math test, I decide that maybe I'm not that stupid after all—until I get to the word problems. I leave that section blank and go back to the office.

Ema and the little fairy godmother are chatting and laughing. No more mascara jokes, I hope.

They both want to hear how the tests went. I don't share my new realization that I'm dumber than I used to be back home.

"Looks like all we have left is to choose an elective," the fairy says. "Let me check."

She looks at her computer.

"I want art," I say. The only subject I'm going to be good at here.

"Hmmmm, sorry," the counselor fairy says. "The kids chose their electives at the end of last year. Looks like at this point the only elective available is band."

Band? I've never played an instrument in my life. And I have a broken arm.

Ema looks at me. I tighten my jaw to keep the tears from coming.

"Have you ever played an instrument before?" She looks at me, then at Ema.

"No," we both say at the same time.

"Well, all levels are welcome, and you're in for a treat. Our school is known for its award-winning band, and Mr. Belton gets chosen 'Teacher of the Year' every year." She gets up in a *we're done here* sort of way.

She shakes Ema's hand. "So happy to have you here with us. So dangerous in Israel."

Ema's lips twitch in a weird way. She looks at me, then back at this good-for-nothing-non-fairy-wicked-witch-of-the-west-coast. "Actually, it's my husband's job that brought us here," she says.

She bites her twitchy lips like she's trying hard not to say anything else.

* * *

"*So dangerous in Israel.*" Ema imitates the counselor on the way to the car. I can tell she's annoyed. She only imitates people if she's annoyed by them. "In this country, anyone can buy an automatic gun, and she thinks it's more dangerous in Israel." She adds a "Ha!" Not the laughing type, the angry type. Loud. With lots of air coming out.

"How nice that you'll be playing an instrument." She switches her tone when we get into the car.

I preferred the angry version. It was much more believable.

"I don't want to play an instrument!" I snap. "They can't make me. Art is the only thing I'm good at."

"You can make art on your own. You're creative enough to come up with your own projects," Ema says. "Playing an instrument will open up a whole new world to you. Music is a language, and you have an opportunity to learn. I think it's great that they offer that in school."

"A new world? A new language? How many new worlds and languages do you think I can take all at once?"

Ema is silent for a while. Eventually she says, "Come on, let's think of an art project we can do together. How about we start with your cast?"

I look out the window. I don't answer her, but I have an idea.

Ema might not like it, but I'm going to do it anyway.

CHAPTER 5

ANGRY BIRDS, ANGRY ME, AND ACRYLIC OCEAN

Ema calls Abba to tell him we're on the way to pick up Gili and asks him to bring her down to the entrance. Apparently, she doesn't want to come upstairs to meet his avocado crew. Meeting the school counselor must've been enough for her.

We pull into a wide parking lot and look for Suite 103. In front of the glass door is a group of people holding signs with bold drawings of scary skulls and poison bottles. They're chanting "Say no to GMO, say no to GMO."

Abba shoves Gili into the car and shuts the door. He waves a mix of goodbye and *you'd better go* and makes his way back into the building through the posters and the protesters.

"They're selling cookies! Like Kay-Lee's." Gili jumps up and down.

"Geez, Gili. Really? Does it look like they are selling cookies?"

Gili presses her face to the window. "You're right,

they look too mad to be selling cookies. Why are they so mad?"

"Ema? What was that all about?" I also want to know.

Ema pulls out of the parking lot. "Nothing you need worry about, girls."

I hate that answer. It usually means that there actually *is* something to worry about. I'll have to google it later.

Ema glances back at Gili, like she's making sure her seatbelt is fastened. "So, tell us, how was it at Abba's office, Gili?"

"It was boring. I didn't understand what anybody was saying except *avocado*. Gibberish, gibberish, gibberish, avocado, gibberish, gib, gib, gibberish, avocado."

"Isn't that the truth," Ema says, laughing. "When you don't understand a language but there's one word that is the same in your language, it sticks out."

"But I got to play Angry Birds on the computer, and some lady gave me colored pencils to draw." She waves a paper between me and Ema.

It's a drawing of avocado-shaped angry birds.

"That's great, Gili," Ema says.

It is pretty good, actually. Maybe annoying little Gili has more in common with me than big blue eyes. Maybe I should let her in on my plan. It will also be the best way to keep her from tattling on me.

"I'm going to my room," I say when we get home. "Gili, come on."

Gili runs up the stairs. She beats me to my room and flops on the bed. I wish I could do that. I'll have to remember to appreciate bed-flopping when my cast is off.

"Here, open this." I hand Gili the box of new brushes that Abba bought me.

I grab the acrylic package and hold it under my cast, using my good arm to rip it open.

"Can I draw with you?" Gili strokes the paint-brushes with her little fingers.

"Sure." I sharpen a pencil.

"We need paper," Gili says.

"Well, no . . ." I say.

Gili's eyes widen. "Are we drawing on your cast?"

"Maybe later," I say. "But first we're going to draw on the wall."

"Really?" Gili's eyes grow bigger and bluer. "Ema will be mad."

"I'll take my chances. Besides, she's the one who got me thinking of this in the first place."

"She did?"

"Sort of. So, are you in?" I ask.

"Ohhh-kayyyy," she says.

"I'll draw in pencil, and you can fill in. We're making an ocean mural."

I start at the bottom corner.

Gili is still nodding like a bobblehead doll. Her eyes look like they might pop out of her head and roll onto the floor.

After lining the bottom with a row of seaweed, I grab the tube of green paint. I have to use my teeth to unscrew the cap. *You can break your teeth like that.* Ema's voice is in my head.

I sniff it. It's a bad smell that brings back good memories. My art teacher at the Tel Aviv Museum used to say that it smells like a wet dog. Mixed with chemicals maybe. Each color smells a little different to me. Anyway, Motek smells much worse than acrylics when he gets wet.

I mix the green with some white to make it lighter. "Here." I hand Gili the paint with a small paintbrush. "Try to stay in the lines." I don't mind if she goes outside the lines a little. I plan to outline everything with black anyway.

Gili's expression changes from *Is she really letting me do this?* to *I'm on an important mission to save the world.*

"Just be careful not to get any paint on the carpet, or Ema will be really mad."

"It's going to be so beautiful. She'll want us to draw all over the house."

Six-year-olds are so naive.

Above the seaweeds, I draw big fish and small fish, fat fish and long fish, all swimming in different directions. I'm kind of inspired by Dr. Seuss's fish, but I'm making them my own, with Gili's expression in their eyes.

"Are you nervous about going to school?" I ask.

Gili's brushstrokes slow to a stop. The look in her eyes changes. Now it's what my fish would look like if there was a shark on my mural.

She's starting first grade. I remember how scary that was. And I knew the language and had my friends from kindergarten. Gili is going to school alone.

I take the brush out of Gili's hand and lay it on the color palette. I hold her hand. It's soft and chubby and warm. "You're going to be just fine, Gili. You're smart and sweet, and I'm sure you'll learn English quickly and make lots of friends." I just said that? It sounded like something Ema would say, and I wouldn't buy it. Does Gili?

"Okay." She pulls her hand out of mine and picks up the paintbrush. "Let's just paint."

"Sure." I pick up my pencil. I add an octopus, a starfish, and a seahorse.

I start singing a song about a girl who loves the sea. Gili joins. I add bubbles going from the fishes' mouths all the way up to the light switch. I accidentally hit the switch with my cast. "Ooooops." I turn the light back on.

The brush flips out of my hand and onto the ground. A light blue stain forms on the ugly beige carpet.

"Ahhhhh!" Gili panics. "Ema's going to be mad."

"Mad about what?" Ema walks in. "Oh. My. God. Shai! What are you doing?"

"Decorating my room," I say, "with my little helper." They never get mad at Gili.

"Oren!" Ema yells to Abba, who just walked in from work. "You have to come up here."

"Are we in trouble?" Gili asks. I keep painting the octopus.

"Stop it right now, Shai. Of course you're in trouble. Wait till Abba sees this."

"You made us come here." I wave my brush in the air. "You call this place home when it isn't. I have no friends to sign my cast. I hate everything here, and you don't even care. Gili's starting first grade and she barely knows English. I can't even take an art class at that horrible school. At least let me have my art on my wall, in *my* room. You're the one who said I should find a way to do art on my own."

"It's beautiful." I hear Abba before I see him.

I turn my head. He's standing at the entrance to my room, staring at the wall.

"What? You're not mad?" Gili asks.

"I am mad," Abba says. "This is not our house. We are renting it. And it's going to be tough to get rid of your artwork. But it's beautiful."

Ema sighs. "It is beautiful."

"If we move out of here, I'll gladly get rid of it myself," I say. "But can I *please* keep it as long as we're here? Please?"

"Please," Gili says.

Ema and Abba look at each other.

"Can we paint a picture on the wall in my room too?" Gili asks. Oh, brother.

"No," Ema says.

If Saba and Safta agree to take me back to Israel with them, Gili can move into this room.

"So can we finish this one?" Gili asks. This is the sweetness I was counting on.

"Yes," Ema says, but it's really thanks to Abba, who's trying to be extra nice about bringing us here. Might as well take advantage of that.

"You'll have to cover the carpet, though," she adds.

I step on the light blue stain.

Ema takes apart a few cardboard boxes left from unpacking and helps us cover the carpet. Afterward, she stays in the room watching us finish. She takes a picture of Gili and me working and another of the wall itself when it's done.

"You should sign your names at the bottom corner," Abba says. So we do.

I take a picture of my new mural and send it to my friends in Israel. It's nighttime there now, but they'll see it when they wake up.

CHAPTER 6

FRENCH TOAST, HOME POOL, AND ALMOST SCHOOL

I wake up to the smell of French toast. I almost forget where I am for a moment, until I drop one foot out of bed and feel the dreadful carpet. I pull it back under the covers.

My bed here is huge and comfy, and I want to love it, but that would be disloyal to my bed back home, so I do my best to hate it. It's a little hard to hate these soft light-blue sheets, though. We all got new bedding sets because the bed sizes are different here.

Ema kept her promise last night, but with just the four of us around the table, it was a sad excuse of Shabbat dinner. I missed Friday nights at Safta's even more.

"What do you girls want to do this weekend?" Abba asks over leftover-challah French toast.

The two-day weekend is the only great thing about this place. My friends in Israel were so jealous when I told them there's no school here on Sunday. Personally, I'd rather go back to my old six-days-a-week school and not be here.

"We want to do absolutely nothing," I say in answer to Abba's question. Although I do need to google what caused the protests in front of his workplace.

Abba and Ema look at each other. "I think the girls need some time to just relax before school starts," Ema says.

"Can I invite a friend to our pool?" Gili asks.

"What friend?" I snap. Does she even realize? "We don't have friends here."

"Let's invite Dora!"

"I think Dora's name is Zoe," I say. Not sure about the idea. Don't we just want to be with each other and not have to speak English, at least on the weekend?

"What an excellent idea!" Abba says. "The neighbor girls probably go to the same schools as you."

"Knowing someone on the first day makes a big difference," Ema says.

The way she dresses, I'm not sure Kay-Lee is the best person to know on my first day when I might already be considered weird myself.

Gili flies out of the kitchen, slamming the front door behind her.

"Is she really going to knock on the neighbors' door by herself just like that?"

"That's our Gili," Abba says. He sounds annoyingly proud.

I'm just as friendly as Gili, or at least I used to be.

"How is she going to invite them? She doesn't even speak English," I say.

Ema is watching Gili from the window. "She's still knocking on the door. She probably needs to ring the doorbell. I'll go help her."

After a few minutes, they come back. Zoe is with them, dressed in a Minnie Mouse swimsuit. She's holding Ema's hand tightly.

"Kay-Lee left early with her father. She helps him at his bakery," Ema says.

"Look, Shai," Gili says, "we brought Dora. Let's take a picture with her."

"She's a real person," I say, "and it's not nice to speak Hebrew in front of her."

"But I don't know English," Gili says.

"She'll teach you," I say, trying not to laugh. Dora the Explorer teaches English on TV in Israel. I wonder what she teaches here.

"She doesn't speak," Gili says.

I look at Ema. Zoe-Dora is still holding her hand.

Ema nods. "I didn't ask why, but her grandmother seemed pleasantly surprised that she wanted to come over. I was hoping Gili will have a chance to improve her English. Oh well."

At the rate Gili's babbling, it's more likely our Dora neighbor will be learning Hebrew.

I go up to my room and grab my laptop. I type the

three letters—*O, M, G*—in the order Gili says them. Object management group? That doesn't make sense. I keep googling . . . ahhh! It's an acronym for Oh My God. So that's why Kay-Lee laughed when Gili called her cookies that? Or is that what she calls her legendary cookies? Anyway, it's not what the protests were about for sure. I enter *G, M, O*. Yes, of course—that's what the signs said. It rhymed with their "say no" song. And there it is: genetically modified organisms. That's what Abba is doing. I feel the blood draining down from my head. I scroll down, looking for more evidence that my father dragged us halfway across the world to participate in playing God.

Words blur in front of my eyes and float around my head, circling me like I'm one of those cartoon characters who got hit on the head: *Toxic. Allergenic. Risks . . . altering ecosystems . . . unintended consequences . . .*

I close my eyes, but the words won't go away. I press my good hand to my eyelids and shut the laptop.

OMG, GMO.

CHAPTER 7

HORRIBLE, MISERABLE, TERRIBLE FIRST DAY OF SCHOOL

"French toast!" Ema calls from downstairs.

On Monday? Either we have lots of leftover challah or else she thinks the first day of school is some special occasion.

"Good luck today, girls." Abba kisses us on the tops of our heads and leaves for work. I can't even look at him.

I manage a few bites of French toast, but the rest won't go down my throat. My arm hurts, but the pain of starting school is going to be worse. I don't take the Advil Ema offers me.

I grab my sketchbook so I can draw places where I'd rather be and disappear between the pages.

Gili is wearing her favorite dress, but she's biting her nails. In the car, she starts crying, and I almost start crying too.

"Don't worry, Gili," Ema says. "I can stay with you for as long as you want. I won't leave until you tell me to. I promise." Gili wipes her tears and stares out the window.

"Are you nervous, Shai?" Ema asks.

"No," I say. I know she doesn't believe me.

Ema and Gili walk into the school with me. None of the other kids have their parents with them. I wish Gili's school started at the same time as mine so that Ema wouldn't have time to hover over me like this.

"You can go," I tell them.

"We can stay with you until the bell rings," Ema says. "I'll help you find your first class."

"Please don't," I say. "I want to do this myself."

Once they leave, I wish they hadn't.

I look around me. A lot of the girls are wearing makeup and nail polish. At my school in Israel, we weren't allowed to wear nail polish. Not that I would anyway.

The bell rings and kids start running in all directions. I start to run too, even though I'm not really sure what direction I should be going.

The pretzels that Ema packed with my lunch are rattling in a plastic box in my backpack.

I get to history class just in time. I sit at the first table near the door.

My heartbeats are louder than the pretzels. I hope I'm the only one hearing them.

I want to pull out my sketchbook, but suddenly I notice that everyone is standing up and staring at me.

Oh. They're not staring at me; they're looking at

the American flag hanging above me.

I stand too. They're all saying a pledge, holding their right hand on their heart. I'm glad mine is broken. My hand, I mean. And my heart? Would I be betraying my country if I do this? I just gaze at the flag, shifting the Star of David on my necklace with my left hand, waiting for the pledge to end.

The blond girl sitting next to me starts talking. It takes me a moment to realize she's talking to me. "I'm a people person," she says, but I don't have a clue what that means.

The teacher is writing on the board. He's talking about "taking notes." I thought notes were just little slips of paper. I'm guessing there's another meaning. Some words are like that. I'm also guessing I'll have to do lots of guessing here. The "taking" part is also weird. Where are we supposed to be taking the notes to?

The voice of my English teacher back home echoes in my head: "In English you 'take' a shower, you 'take' a picture, you 'take' a hike . . ." In Hebrew there's a specific verb for each of these things.

When the bell rings, I rush to my second-period class, in sync with the beat of my rattling pretzels. I find it pretty easily. It's science. I used to like science before my scientist-father brought us here.

The lab looks like a legit lab that real scientists

would have. So cool. I want to take a picture, or maybe draw it.

The teacher is dressed like she's going to a bar mitzvah. "Welcome, scientists," she says. "I'm Mrs. Adams." She sounds like she has a cold, and her eyes and nose are almost as red as her dress.

The blond "people person" is waving to me from the back of the room.

Should I go sit next to her? It's not like I have anyone else to sit with. I walk over and force myself to smile as I sit. She tells me she's just moved here from Virginia and how different it is here. I'm pretty sure Virginia is in the United States. She has no idea what *different* is.

"I'm from Israel," I say. I try not to speak too much, so I won't make too many mistakes.

"Really? Wow. Do you ride camels there?" she asks. I flex my eyeballs hard so they won't roll. I don't answer. I try to follow what the teacher's saying.

Looks like there's a flag next to the door in every class. There's also a phone in every classroom. Must be nice for the teachers to have their own little office in their own classroom. I bet my teachers in Israel would love that. Mrs. Adams has pictures of her kids on her desk.

I pull out my sketchbook and start drawing Mrs. Adams. I use a red colored pencil for the dress and the tip of her nose. The nose, as usual, is the worst part of the drawing. I turn it into a round, circled clown's nose. I add the lab equipment around her. I've never drawn a microscope before, but you can't tell. It looks professional since it doesn't have a nose.

I stare at the American flag for a second and sketch the shape of it in the background, but I color it in as the Israeli flag instead.

* * *

I walk into my next class and scan the classroom looking for People Person. She isn't here. I put myself in robot mode. I figure it's better than feeling like an alien from outer space.

Math is a good class to be in robot mode. I've always been good at math. Numbers are the same in all languages.

But I notice someone looking at me, and he's the cutest boy I've ever seen in my life. His light brown hair falls across his forehead, covering a bit of his left eye. He reminds me of a boy I had a crush on in Israel who used to shake his hair away from his eyes in the same way, but this guy is way cuter. So much for robot mode—robots don't blush.

When our eyes meet, he flicks the hair from his eye, looking down at his paper. He seems so focused on his math. Maybe I imagined he was looking at me.

Lunchtime scares me most of all.

I'm used to the Israeli way—you eat the bagged lunch you bring from home at your desk.

But I've seen the American way on TV. The girl who sits alone at lunch is going to be me.

At this school, there's no cafeteria like I've seen in the movies. Instead there's a shaded area outside with lunch tables. Ema guessed it's because the weather is always nice in San Diego.

I wonder about Kay-Lee, our colorful neighbor. Maybe she doesn't go to this school. Maybe she's homeschooled. I brought up the idea of homeschooling, but Abba and Ema were both against it. Abba said the whole point is to improve our English and social skills, to be exposed to a new culture. I thought the point was his oh-so-amazing job opportunity.

Kids burst into the lunch area, like people at the airport hurrying to catch their flights. It's way more terrifying than I imagined.

I don't see People Person, so I go over to a table where I spot a girl sitting alone. "Can I sit here?" I ask.

"Sure," she says, but she doesn't look up.

After a few minutes, a group of girls join her. They all ignore me, like I'm not even there. Their bought lunch smells disgusting. I eat my hummus sandwich and my pretzels.

I ask them if they know where the gym is, and they point right behind me. The gym is a few steps from the lunch area, which makes me seem stupid. I'm so stupid here.

I get up and go toward the gym, even though the bell didn't ring yet. Now that I've eaten my pretzels, I miss their rattling sound.

I peek through the open doors of the gym. It's ginormous. I want to go in and shout. There must be an awesome echo in there, but I can't even make myself walk in.

The bell rings and kids scatter in all directions. Feels like I'm at the airport again, alone, and about to miss my flight.

The PE teacher, Mr. Holt, calls attendance, and I'm not on his list. I raise my hand and tell him so.

"Are you sure you're in this class?" he asks.

"Yes." I memorized the rest of the day after science class.

"My name is Shai." My voice is trembling. I don't sound like myself. Who am I?

"Welcome, Shai. I see you have a broken arm, so I'm guessing you won't be able to participate in PE for a while. Do you have a note from the nurse?"

A note. He means a permission slip. Why would he

need a note? Can't he see for himself I can't participate?

"Shai?" Mr. Holt pulls me out of my thoughts. "Do you know where the health office is?"

I can't even find my voice; how will I be able to find the nurse's office? I slowly move my head from side to side, looking down.

"Who can show Shai to the health office?" Mr. Holt asks.

"I'll go, Mr. Holt." A loud voice comes from the back of the class.

I turn around and see my weird neighbor, dressed in an odd mixture of colorful patterns.

"Thank you, Kay-Lee," Mr. Holt says.

"Sure thing," Kay-Lee says.

* * *

"Hey, neighbor," Kay-Lee says as we walk out of the classroom. "I was wondering if we'd have any classes together."

I was too. But I don't say anything.

"You know, I've never met anyone from Israel before. You don't look like someone who would be from Israel."

And you look like my sister's breakfast, I almost say. "How do you think someone from Israel should look?"

"I don't know . . . I'm not sure. Never mind.

I guess you just looked American to me, until I heard your accent."

Kay-Lee adjusts her Froot-Loop-colored headband and points at my cast. "What happened?"

"Stair surfing," I say.

She laughs and doesn't ask anything else, which I appreciate. Her laughter rings like wind chimes. "You and your sister are funny. I loved that she called the non-GMO cookies OMG cookies—that's genius. I've officially renamed snickerdoodles OMG-cookies."

I try to fake a smile, but my whole face freezes.

"The health office is right around the corner." She points. "I guess I should get back to class now. See you around, Shai."

* * *

The health office smells like a blend of medicine and mint.

"How can I help you, sweetie?" the nurse asks. She's bandaging some guy's forehead. Looks like someone was aiming for his eye and missed.

"Um, I broke my arm, um, not now, but um, I can't do PE, and Mr. Holt said he needs a note from you."

"That's correct, sweetie, and I need a note from your physician, stating your condition and estimating how long you won't be able to exercise."

Notes, notes, notes. I want to call Ema, but . . . I can't remember her American cell number. I can't remember the home number either.

"Is everything all right, sweetie?" the nurse asks. I wish she'd stop calling me sweetie.

"Yes, um, no, I, um." What's wrong with me? I can't even speak basic English now.

"We're new here, everything is new. I can't remember anything. And I want to call my mom."

She pulls out a folder. "It's all on file, sweetie. Let's see." She puts on yellow glasses, the shade of honey, which match her *sweetie* theme. "There it is. Neta Epstein. Correct?"

"Yes," I say. The bandaged guy gives me a look like I'm the one who just punched him and stares at my necklace.

"Okay then. I'm dialing . . . I hope she answers. There are no emergency contacts on the form besides your parents' numbers."

We don't know anyone here! I want to yell.

"Mrs. Epstein? Hi. This is Nurse Stacey calling from San Elijah Middle School. I have sweet Shai here with me in my office—oh, nothing to worry about. I'm going to need a physician's note about her broken arm. She wants to talk to you. I'm handing the phone over to her, sweetie."

Did she just call Ema "sweetie" too?

"Heefhida otach?" I ask Ema. Bandage Boy gives me the kind of look you give someone who doesn't pick up after their dog.

The nurse stares at me too. So what? It feels good to be able to talk to Ema without anyone around understanding.

"Yes. She scared me. I thought something happened to you. What's all this about a note from the doctor? Can't she see your cast? Why didn't the counselor say anything about this?"

"I don't know, Ema." I thought talking to her would make me feel better, but she's only making it worse. "I have to go now. Just . . . please call the doctor's office and get me that permission slip." I hang up and close my eyes for a second to convince my tears to go back in.

I pull out my schedule. I forgot the room number for language arts.

Oh no.

My stomach shrinks, dribbling against the walls of my insides. I was supposed to be in language arts this period. PE comes after. No wonder I wasn't on the roll call list.

I suck in my cheeks and feel my jaw shiver. The tears are coming, and nothing can stop them. Nurse Sweetie hands me a tissue on my way out.

I go back to the gym and tell Mr. Holt that I've

mixed up my classes. "Well, worse things have been known to happen," he says. "Stay here until the bell rings. No harm done in switching just for today. Tomorrow, stick to your schedule."

* * *

"Well, that's unfortunate," the language arts teacher says when I tell her what happened. "I do recall marking you absent from the previous period." She looks around the room. All the seats are taken.

"This is an honors class," she says. "Let's see . . . You can sit here for today." She rolls a chair that's like hers, with wheels, not like the chairs the kids have. She places it right next to her. Facing the kids.

Can this day get any worse? I have no idea what "honors class" means, but it sounds like something advanced, something I'd probably be in if I'd been born here.

I sit in that rolling chair and all eyes are on me. Maybe I'm right under the flag again. No. It's on the other side, near the door. They're staring at me.

There's an empty seat in the back. I could have at least pulled out my sketchbook if the teacher had let me sit there. Her voice becomes a constant buzzing background for my *I don't belong here* thoughts. I'll listen to her tomorrow. Maybe.

My body feels heavy, but I have to drag myself to one last period: band.

* * *

People Person is in this class. So is the cute boy from my math class. I lower my gaze. I listen closely as names are called. Not just to hear that I'm in the right class—I'm sure I am—but to know what *his* name is.

People Person's name is Jenny. Cutest Boy on Earth's name is Chris.

Mr. Belton tells us to look around at the instruments and pick them up, feel them, see if we connect to any of them. The saxophone looks cool, but with the cast on one hand, I can't even lift it. Some kids already have an instrument that they brought with them. I look at Chris. He pulls a trumpet out of his case. I walk to the trumpet on display. Maybe I'll try that.

Mr. Belton comes over to me and says, "The trumpet is a pretty good instrument for beginners. You can hold it with your left hand. Why don't you try it?"

I bring it to my mouth and blow.

The sound comes out much louder than I expected. Everybody looks at me.

"Pretty good," Mr. Belton says. "Now, if you can manage moving the fingers of your broken arm, you should be fine."

"She's from Israel. She doesn't speak much English," says Jenny.

So that's what a "people person" is? Someone telling people about a person that they don't even know themselves?

"The only language we need to know here," Mr. Belton says, "is the language of music. What's your name again?" he asks me.

"Shai."

"Okay, Shy Butterfly. Seems like the cast is a challenge you'll overcome, and once it's off, you will spread both wings and fly into the wonderful world of music. Now, all of you, if you don't have an instrument already, choose the instrument that is calling out your name. Grab it and come sit down."

I stare at the musical notes, and even though I don't know how to read them yet, it comforts me to know that like numbers, they are the same all around the world.

Mr. Belton talks about rules and regulations, same as in the other classes, but he uses the triangle and the tambourine as he speaks. He hits the drum every once in a while, to match what he's saying.

When the bell rings, everybody rushes out.

First day is over. It felt like a year.

I look around me. The band room is almost empty. Only a few kids are still packing their instruments.

"Bye-bye, Shy-Shy," Jenny chirps from the doorway.

Why am I still standing here?

"Don't worry, Shy Butterfly, you'll be fine," Mr. Belton's voice interrupts my thoughts. "By winter break, you won't even remember you were once the new kid."

I wish I could believe him.

CHAPTER 8

GMo, CHEESE STICK, AND LANGUAGE FARTS

"So how was the first day of school?" Abba asks.

I sigh. Gili has a mouth full of schnitzel.

"Come on, girls, give me one word," Abba is begging.

"Nightmare," I whisper.

"Fun," Gili says, her mouth still loaded with food.

"I'm glad to hear that, Gili," Abba says, hearing only what he wants to hear.

"I'm sure tomorrow will be better for you, Shai," Ema says. "It takes time to adjust to a new place."

"Everything is delicious, Neta," Abba says to Ema, changing the subject. "How about some wine? Let's raise a toast."

Is he serious?

"To what?" I shout.

"To our life in America, to the beginning of the school year, and to the gene responsible for oxidation that I found in the avocado today!" Abba exclaims, getting a bottle of wine and two wine glasses.

"Oxy-what?" Gili asks.

"Oxidation. It's the chemical process that causes avocados to brown. I'm on my way to finding a solution to neutralize it."

He really thinks he's saving the world. I'm not hungry anymore. "You're genetically modifying avocados and you think it's something to celebrate?"

"Where is this coming from?" Abba asks and takes a sip of his wine making the most annoying slurp sounds.

"You're interfering with nature. Why do you think you can play God? Our neighbors make non-GMO cookies and here you are next door, adding more GMO to the world. And you're proud of it." I get up.

Abba puts his wine glass down.

"It's those protesters . . ." Ema starts saying.

"Those biotech foes spreading misinformation." Abba sighs. "Most of them don't understand what it is they're against."

"It's all true!" I yell. "I read about it online."

"Calm down," Abba says, which makes me way less calm. "It's more complex than you think." That's what adults say when they don't feel like explaining. "GMO is a tool, an advanced tool that can benefit mankind. And yes, it could be problematic if not used responsibly. But you have to be very careful about generalizing.

I'm glad you're showing interest—I'd love to tell you more . . ."

Well, he is explaining, but I'm not interested in his explanations. "I'm going to take a shower." I grab my plate and storm to the sink to clear it.

My fork falls in with my leftovers. I turn on the garbage disposal—the perfect sound effect.

"Shai!" Ema shouts.

I turn it off and pull out what's left of the beaten-up fork. It looks like I feel.

"Do you need help washing your hair?" Ema asks.

I forgot I can't do that myself with the broken arm. "Please," I say—mostly to my tears, begging them to not show up.

In the bathroom, Ema washes my hair in silence, her hands massaging my scalp through the warm water. I wipe away warm tears.

"It will get easier," Ema says.

"Okay," I say, because she sounds like she's about to cry too. "It's just the shampoo in my eyes."

* * *

I wake up to a new day with great wavy curls.

Second day of horror—horrible waste of a good hair day.

Gili is wearing the outfit she wore on her birthday.

She's twirling around the living room, singing the ABC song. Motek is running around her, sniffing under her skirt.

"Stop it," she says. In English.

"Speak Hebrew with him," I tell her.

"He understands English." Gili giggles. "He's a smart dog."

"We're Hebrew speakers in this house!" I bang my fist on the kitchen table.

"Shai." Ema puts her hand on my fist.

Now even Motek is American. I hate it.

Gili sings the English alphabet song all the way to school, which makes me want to chop my ears off, but I don't say anything. It's a short ride.

At least she and Ema don't get out of the car with me today.

There are so many kids in this school, from so many ethnicities. I love that.

I think of Kay-Lee. Yesterday I was offended when she said I don't look Israeli, but honestly if she had moved to my school in Israel, I would've thought she was Asian, not American. I've never met any Asians in Israel, and there are so many here, but they are Americans too.

"Hi, Shai. Hey, that rhymes!"

I look behind me. It's Jenny. She doesn't know anyone here either, but she's a different type of "new kid." She's not *that* different. She's like a fruit in a bowl of vegetables. Some fruits are even mistaken for vegetables, like avocados. Ugh. Couldn't some other image pop into my mind now? The point is, she can fit in eventually. But me—I'm more of a cheese stick. Taken out of a totally different food group. Too different to ever blend in.

"Shai? Hi," Jenny says again.

"Oh, hi."

The image of myself as a lonely cheese stick in a vegetable salad is still blinking in my head.

We walk together to first-period history and sit next to each other.

"I love your hair," Jenny says. "How do you curl it like that?"

"I don't," I answer, realizing how that sounded only after the words have left my mouth, hating that I seem so standoffish.

The bell rings. I hope Jenny doesn't talk as much as she did yesterday during class—I don't want to get in trouble.

The first two hours feel like two months. I keep looking back and forth from the board to the paper, trying not to make any spelling mistakes. My good arm hurts more than the broken one, and my writing is getting smeared.

I used to only smear math, since Hebrew is written from right to left. There are no perks to being a lefty here.

"Let's sit together at lunch. I couldn't find you yesterday," Jenny says when the bell rings. "I'll be on the far-left side of the gym."

There's a chance this day will be better than yesterday after all. At least today, I won't be eating lunch alone. I decide to try to like Jenny, even though I might not have become friends with her in my real world where my real friends are.

I skip to the beat of the pretzels on my back. I never imagined I'd find comfort in the sound of rattling pretzels. I'll have to remember not to eat them all at lunch.

I slow down as I get closer to my math class. Chris is standing at the door joking around with Bandage Boy from the nurse's office. Chris smiles when I walk in. I wish I could smile back, but my mouth freezes instead.

"Hey, you're from Israel, right?" Chris asks when I sit down.

My head defrosts just enough to nod, but my mouth is still in deep freeze.

"Cool," he says. "The land of the first USB flash drive."

Bandage Boy rolls his eyes and slaps the back of Chris's head. "You're such a nerd," he says as he walks to his seat.

"Really," Chris goes on, "Israel is one of the most technologically advanced countries in the world."

"True." One word somehow comes out of my frozen mouth. I wish I'd said, *Thank you for being educated* or *Thank you for not asking if we ride camels.* But the bell rings, and Chris goes to his seat. I want to concentrate on math, but my mind chooses to concentrate on the cute, smart, Israel-appreciating Chris.

At lunchtime, I look for Jenny at the tables outside, but she's not there. I guess it's a longer walk from her class. I look around. Color strikes my vision. So much color on one person. My eyes hurt. The color wheel waves to me, and I recognize it's Kay-Lee. I wave back.

She kind of weakens my vegetable-salad theory. She's sort of a cheese stick herself. And she's also sitting alone. Maybe I should go sit with her . . .

"Hi, Shai. Oh my, Shai. I'm so hungry I could die, Shai." Jenny. She's surrounded by four giggling girls. "Shai, meet my friends from math class." She waves her hand like Mr. Belton does when he's conducting the band. "Madison, Olivia, Mia, and Mikaela."

"Hi, Shai," they all say together, perfectly orchestrated by Jenny.

"Isn't that so fun to say? Hi, Shai. Bye, Shai," Jenny squeals. They all sit. I guess I'm stuck here.

"I wish you were in our math class," Jenny says to me.

I don't. I have enough classes with her.

Madison, or is it Mia? One of the M's—I can't tell the difference—takes a loud bite off a huge apple. "Jenny sat next to the clown girl in math. She could hardly concentrate with all that color beside her. Right, Jenny?" she asks with her mouth full. "Have you seen her, Shai?"

"My gosh," Jenny says. "What a freak. Shai, you should see her."

I glance in Kay-Lee's direction.

"That's her! Circus clown," one of the M's says. "She's been dressing like that ever since her mom left a few years ago."

"Yesterday was worse—stripes and dots," says the M with the apple, spritzing apple juice around her.

"How horrible," Jenny says. "Why would anyone choose to dress like that?"

Why do people always think there has to be a reason for everything? Maybe that's just how she likes to dress. I can't just sit here and say nothing. "You have to admire her for wearing whatever she likes and not caring what other people think."

Olivia smiles an almost invisible smile. She seems

so gentle, like she's made of air. She's the only one whose name doesn't start with an M and the only one with dark hair. She's wearing the same Converse shoes as I am. I imagine her floating on a cloud, which would explain why her shoes are in much better shape than mine.

The M with the apple throws what's left of it toward a trash can—and misses. "You think it's a fashion statement?"

I stare at the partially eaten apple on the floor. "Well, it might be," I say. She's braver than I am: She's different by choice. "And yesterday wasn't that bad," I add, even though it was really bad.

"You saw her yesterday?" Jenny asks.

"Yes. She was in my PE class. I mean, she isn't in my scheduled PE class. Only yesterday, um . . . I went to the wrong class, by mistake."

"Really?" One of the M's opens her mouth so big I can see all her teeth. I wish a bug would fly right into it.

"That is *so* embarrassing," Jenny says. "I would die, Shai. Die-Shy. That rhymes too."

I almost yell, "Die, Jenny!" But, of course, I don't. It would sound bad if I didn't explain, and I'm not in the mood to give a Hebrew lesson right now.

I check my schedule to make sure I get it right today—even though I'm sure I'll never get it wrong again. Language arts. Fancy name for English class, and the closest I'm ever going to get to art in this school.

"Hey," Olivia says, "so we have language arts together. The teacher did call out 'Shay' a bunch of times at roll call yesterday, so you'll have to correct her pronunciation. That's probably annoying. I think we have PE together too."

She noticed. I like her.

"Aren't you in a class for English learners?" Jenny asks.

"This school doesn't offer it. I'm in regular English—I mean Language *Farts*." They all laugh.

I hope they got that it was a joke and not an English-learner mistake.

It stinks having to doubt my own sense of humor.

"That was intended, right?" says the M with the juicy apple.

"Was *that* intended?" I point at her partially eaten apple next to the trash can.

She shrugs but walks over and picks it up.

CHAPTER 9

BUTTERFLIES, PAINTBRUSHES, AND A PINK TUTU

When I bring in Dr. Lorax's note, Nurse Sweetie is smiling so wide that she looks like she's advertising toothpaste. I stare at her white, straight teeth as she tells me I should be in PE class this week after all. "Come back to my office next week, sweetie," she says, "when the actual exercising starts."

Turns out there's no real PE in the beginning. You don't even change into PE clothes.

Everyone's watching a movie when I get to the gym. It's all boring rules and regulations about PE. Afterward, Mr. Holt talks about the importance of physical education. A crease between his eyes deepens. When he's done explaining, he takes out a pile of papers and says, "Chris." The crease between his eyes straightens, and so do I. Is he referring to the Chris I think he is?

"Yes, Mr. Holt."

Yes, it's *the* Chris, and I'm definitely in the right PE class.

"Can you help me pass out these forms, please?" Mr. Holt asks.

Chris gets up. He flicks his hair out of his eyes. My stomach flips.

"Hakim, please help Chris," Mr. Holt says. It's Bandage Boy, without the bandage. I'm glad Chris starts handing out the forms on the left side of the room, where I'm sitting.

When he hands me a form, he says, "Voicemail technology was also developed in Israel."

I smile. I didn't know that, but I believe him. I take the paper from his hand.

First name, last name. Pretty easy so far. I don't have a middle name, though. I wonder if all Americans do. I leave that part blank. Date—I have to remind myself that you put the month before the day here.

The first question is, *What do you most look forward to in PE?* That would be easy to answer if I were back home. Being with my friends. I sigh. Probably a bit too loudly.

The girl sitting to my left stares at me. I look back down at the form. What do I look forward to? I don't see the point of this question. I leave it blank.

Next question: *Do you participate in any extracurricular activities?* I stare at that long word. No clue what it means. Outer space comes to mind. I stare into space.

Hakim collects the forms from my side. I'm glad

it isn't Chris. I wouldn't want him to notice I haven't completed mine.

I smile at Hakim, but he doesn't smile back, and he doesn't look at my blank form. He looks straight into my eyes, then down to my Star of David for a split second before looking away. He doesn't like me. When he takes the forms from the girls sitting next to me, he smiles. His face lights up when he does. He's pretty cute. I look at Chris collecting forms on the other side—much cuter.

When the bell rings, I rush to band.

"Hello, Shy Butterfly," Mr. Belton greets me when I walk in.

"Hi, you little butterfly." I turn around. Jenny. She just ruined "Shy Butterfly" for me. Now I hope Mr. Belton never calls me that again.

"Musicians—take your spots," Mr. Belton says.

The cool metal of the trumpet feels good in my hand. But not as good as holding a paintbrush.

We are working on two notes. Tomorrow Mr. Belton will add the third. It really is a new language, but I like it because it's new to everyone. We are all learning it together.

When the bell rings, I go put the trumpet in its case. I stroke the metal before I shut it. I really can do art on my own, and Mr. Belton gave me an idea for my cast.

Ema has taken Gili to try a ballet class. I'm home alone and done with my homework. I look down at my blank cast, dirty around the edges. It's time.

I pull out the acrylics and brushes from under my bed. I've used up a lot of the new paint on the mural, but there's still enough. I won't ask for more—I won't give Abba the satisfaction of knowing how much I love them. I choose the thinnest brushes. I just need a little water for mixing. I'd better not do this in my room, though—there's already one permanent blue stain on the carpet.

I go downstairs. Motek follows me to the kitchen as I grab a plastic cup and fill it with water.

Outside by the pool I set everything on the little table next to the lounge chair. I line up the different shades of blue. Next, I add white and black to the lineup. And purple and green.

Motek rushes behind me and jumps into the pool. He definitely likes his life as a dolphin. Living in denial. I watch him swim laps.

I check my phone for images of butterflies. It's easier to copy than to draw from my imagination. I'm a good copier. That always feels a little like cheating, though. But I copy from photos, not from another artist's drawings, so I guess it's okay.

I scroll down for clear images. I love the patterns of monarch butterflies. I'll base my drawing on their shape and patterns even though they're orange and my butterflies will all be blue. As I look at the pictures, I catch a glimpse of text. Three specific letters jump at me: G, M, O.

"A new study concludes that monarch butterflies may become extinct within two decades . . . herbicides used with genetically modified corn spread and kill the milkweed plants where monarchs lay their eggs . . ."

I have to show Abba. Does he know? Doesn't he care?

I put down my phone and start drawing, from my head. I'll let myself be distracted by art for now.

I start with pencil, like I always do. I don't want any background. I want the whole cast filled with butterflies—wings overlapping. It's hard to find a comfortable position with the cast. I balance the water cup between my knees.

Motek swims back and forth like he's practicing for the Olympics. The sound of the water makes me need to go pee, but I have everything set up just right. I don't want to get up until I'm done. I have to keep moving my casted arm to awkward angles, so I can fill in the whole thing. I should have brought a mirror. Oh, well. I'll just skip the area under the armpit for now.

I wonder if everybody does that, not only in art, but life in general—save the hard parts for later and deal with what's easy first. Abba should be smart enough to start with what's hard. But he's ignoring the hard. Being in a business that kills butterflies, choosing his career over his family. Will he ever realize how hard it is for me?

"Shai! Shai!" Gili twirls into the backyard. "Look what I learned." I didn't even feel that an hour had passed. That's one of the things I love about art.

She's jumping up and down, but when she reaches me, she stops. "Wow! Butterflies. Wait, you said I can help with the cast." I forgot about that.

She flops on the chair next to me. The blue water in my cup quivers.

"Hey, watch it!" I hold on to the cup. "Be careful not to get your pink tutu blue."

Gili frowns. "You promised."

"Okay, look." I lift my arm and show her the blank spot that I couldn't reach.

"No one is going to see it. It's under your armpit." Gili crosses her arms over her chest.

"So it can be a private drawing just for me," I say.

She twirls her pigtails for a second before dropping her hands to her sides. She's kind of cute for an annoying little sister.

"Take off your tutu so you don't get paint on it."

She slips out of her tutu skirt and crawls under my arm. She's holding my hand up with one hand and painting with the other. It tickles.

"Don't move," Gili says. "You'll mess it up."

I have a bossy ballerina up my armpit. "I'm trying, but you're tickling me." I also desperately need to pee.

She washes the brush in the cup still clamped between my legs. The water turns a beautiful shade of purplish blue. I want to dump it into the pool, but I doubt half a cup will have any effect on a full pool. Gili switches to green and washes the brush again. Now the water is more of a brownish shade. I won't try my pool experiment with that.

"Done," she declares.

I can't hold it any longer, so I run to the bathroom, my arm up at a ninety-degree angle. "I'm going to see it in the mirror." I land on the toilet right in time. That was close.

Before I get to the mirror to check out Gili's drawing on my cast, I hear her screaming. I run back outside. Motek is swimming with the pink tutu on his head. I burst into laughter. Good thing this didn't happen before I peed. How did it even get on his head? I grab my phone and take a picture.

"It's not funny!" Gili yells.

"It is a little funny." I can't stop laughing. But I think of those TV shows where people send in videos of their kids falling off slides and all sorts of accidents, and it's supposed to be funny, but I always think it's mean. So now I'm the mean person. I do wish I had a video of me surfing down the stairs, though. My friends in Israel would've loved it.

"Sorry, Gili." I stop laughing. "You're right, it's not funny."

She looks at me and then back at Motek in the pool. "Okay, it's a little funny," she says, "but still." She stomps her foot. "I want my tutu back."

"I can't get in with my cast. Go get a treat for him. That will get him out for sure."

She does. Ema follows. The minute she sees Motek, she starts laughing like she's lost her mind. Good thing Gili is busy calling Motek, who sees the treat in her hand and comes right out. Ema takes the tutu off of him, still laughing. I'm glad I took a picture.

"It's just a little wet, Gili." Ema finally tames her wild laughter. "Nothing happened to it." She notices my cast. "Wow, Shai," she says, "that's gorgeous."

Gili puts her tutu on the lounge chair to dry. "Did you see my secret drawing?"

"I was going to," I admit, "but then the Swan Lake Motek Show started."

Gili takes my hand and leads me to the bathroom mirror. I slowly lift my arm.

It's two green caterpillars with purple stripes, a little

green heart in between them with a purple contour. "It's you and me, right before we turn into butterflies," Gili says. I get down on my knees and hug her.

"I love the caterpillar sisters," I say, deciding not to mention there's the cocoon phase before that.

CHAPTER 10

TIE-DYE, LOCKERS, AND AN ENVELOPE FROM OLIVIA

"Shai, wow!" Jenny sounds genuine for a change. "Did you draw that?"

"Yes." A few other girls gather around. I didn't realize my butterfly cast would draw so much attention.

The bell rings. "Nice job on the cast," Mr. Ford says when I enter the history classroom. All these compliments remind me I'm still good at something.

Kay-Lee comes up to me when I get to the lunch area. She looks like a swirly, twisted lollipop in her tie-dye shirt.

"I love your cast," she says. "Did you hire an artist to do that?"

Her question isn't making sense. Isn't "higher" the opposite of "lower"? Maybe it has another meaning. Will English ever get easier? "I did it myself," I say, hoping it answers her question.

"Wow!"

"I wanted to be in art class," I tell her, "but there were no spots left."

"It's not that great," she says. "The teacher is mean and has strict rules. It's only been a few days, but I don't think it's going to be any fun." She points at my cast. "You could probably teach that class."

I smile. "The band teacher is very nice."

"Maybe I should switch to band," Kay-Lee says. "Then we'll be together."

Would she still want that if she knew that Abba is in the business of Frankensteining food?

"Come on, Shai." Jenny and the M's show up. "Look what she drew on her cast," she tells the M's. They all "ooooh" and "ahhhhh" together. Jenny links her arm in mine. "Let's go sit, Shy-Shai."

"Want to sit with us?" I ask Kay-Lee. Jenny and the M's stab me with their looks.

Kay-Lee notices. "It's okay," she says. "I'll see you later." She turns away. I want to say something, but she swirls away so quickly I don't get a chance. Lollipop colors melt into the crowd.

"What was she talking about just now—something about you being together?" Jenny asks with a disgusted expression, like Kay-Lee just gave her food poisoning.

"She was thinking maybe she'd switch her elective to band."

"She'll be in band with us?" Jenny asks. Extra horrible food poisoning face.

"Can you switch at this point?" one of the M's asks.

"There's always room in band," Jenny says.

"So," I ask, "could I possibly ask for her spot in art? I mean, it was full when I came to register, but if she transfers . . ."

"I'm not sure you can do that," Jenny says. Her eyeballs wander side to side, up and down. Her eyebrow twitches. "I have to run to the bathroom before my next class. Catch you all later." She waves like she's the Queen of England and runs off in the opposite direction of the bathrooms.

* * *

We're watching a movie again. Is PE going to be like this all year? It's about how to operate our lockers, which we're getting today.

After the movie, we line up, and eighth graders hand each of us a lock and a card with the combination written on it. Not too complicated. I open my locker in a few seconds.

"How'd you do that so fast, and with a broken arm?" Olivia looks like she's getting into a fist fight with her locker. "Can you open mine?" she asks.

"Sure."

She shows me her numbers. I rotate the dial back and forth. Easy.

"Wow, Shai," Olivia says.

A girl standing next to her says, "Can you open mine too?" And I do.

More girls ask for my help. Turns out I'm a fluent locker opener.

Girls are high-fiving me as I open their lockers.

"You're a pro," Olivia says.

"You'll have to learn how to do that yourselves, you know," one of the eighth graders says.

"She'll probably be able to do them two at a time when her cast is off," her friend says.

"Everyone back to the field," Mr. Holt calls, "we don't have all day."

On the way from the locker rooms, one of the girls tells the boys how I opened their lockers. I wish she didn't.

"Way to go, lock-pro," Chris says. Heat rushes up to my ears. Hakim snorts. He's nice to everyone but me.

"So, new girl found her true calling," one guy laughs.

"Yeah, she'd be a natural bank robber," his friend says.

I wish the ground would open and swallow me whole.

"Ignore them," Olivia says. "Pat and Matt are always looking for trouble.

"Tomorrow, we get moving," Mr. Holt says. "Don't forget your PE uniform."

My broken arm is saving my dignity for a few weeks. Even though Ema adjusted the waistband on the shorts, they still dangle to my knees. The T-shirt hangs like a shapeless dress.

Mr. Holt says the bell is going to ring any minute and lets us hang out on the field until it does.

"How do you spell your name?" Olivia asks.

"S-H-A-I. It's pronounced like being shy. But I'm not shy." Did I just say the exact thing I decided not to say?

"I like it," Olivia says. "It's so original."

"It means *gift* in Hebrew," I add.

"I wish my name had a cool meaning. *Olivia* sounds like olives, but I hate olives."

I smile.

"I've never met anyone from Israel. Does everybody in Israel have such amazing eyes?"

"No." I laugh. She's so much nicer when the M's aren't around.

When the bell rings, Mr. Holt comes up to me and tells me I'll have to go sit in the nurse's office starting next week, until my cast is off.

Inside the locker rooms, Olivia gives me an envelope. It says "Shai" in stylish cursive.

"Hope you can make it. Sorry for the late notice," she says. "Gotta run. My last period is way at the other end of the school."

I look at the beautiful handwriting. That's why she asked how I spell my name.

"Hey, locker pro, don't worry about your English too much—you don't need it to be a safecracker." Pat and Matt call after me as I head toward the band room.

Their laughter rattles in my ears like nails in a rusted tin can. I lock my ears, hold tight to the envelope, and keep walking.

* * *

"Hello, Shy Butterfly," Mr. Belton greets me when I walk into the band room. He looks at my arm. "Butterflies. I see I've inspired you." I smile. He has.

"Who did this wonderful work of art?" he asks.

"I did," I answer and rush to my seat. I peek inside the envelope from Olivia. I'm invited to a sleepover. The band room seems like the right place to be when there's music in my heart.

Jenny turns to me, grinning, the clarinet on her lap. She's mouthing something to me. I hate the exaggerated look of her talking with no sound. I think she's saying, "I have to tell you something." I can't hear her since I'm in the trumpet section in the back and she's in the first row with the clarinets. I shove the envelope from Olivia in my backpack.

Mr. Belton teaches us a way to remember the notes.

Every Good Boy Does Fine: EGBDF. I wonder if this is how it's taught in Israel, or maybe there are words in Hebrew to help remember. Music is my favorite language now. When I concentrate on the music, I don't think of anything else. It's like art. Music *is* art. If Safta and Saba agree to take me back to Israel with them, I'll sign up for trumpet lessons.

CHAPTER 11

FRIDAY, CHALLAH, AND GENERALIZATIONS

I flop on my bed in slow motion. Slow-motion flopping is a new technique I've developed with the cast. With my left hand, I hug the cast on my right and launch myself onto the bed.

"I've been invited to a sleepover," I tell the fish on my wall. They stare at me with their wide-open Gili-eyes.

I check the invitation. Oh. It's tonight. I can't go. Family first on Friday night. We're going to the Levis' for dinner—I hope their girls are more like Lily and less like their obnoxious dad. It would be nice to have a friend who speaks Hebrew. Oh, well. I probably wouldn't fit in at that sleepover anyway.

Ema is baking challah and the house fills with the smell of Shabbat dinner. I miss Safta, but I remind myself she'll be here in two days.

"Finally, Friday," Abba says when he walks in from work.

I thought he loved his job here. Isn't that why we're here in the first place?

* * *

The smell of the challah fills the car, like it's teasing us, telling us we're smelling it in all the wrong places.

"So, anything positive about school today?" Abba asks on the way to the Levis'.

Same question every night. He doesn't give up.

Gili jumps up and down. If it wasn't for the car seat, she'd be in Abba's lap. I keep forgetting to tell her not to act happy. If we both seem miserable, maybe our parents will consider moving back to Israel.

"I have two new friends," she says, "and we all have the same favorite colors. Pink and purple."

Three six-year-olds all loving the same dreadful colors. Easy to find something in common with Americans when you're six. I look out the window thinking of the monarch butterflies.

"How about you, Shai?" Abba asks.

"Just found out you're killing butterflies."

"What?" Abba and Ema say, synchronized. Ema's head spins in my direction so fast I'm surprised she doesn't hurt her neck. Abba keeps his eyes on the road, but I can see him squint in the rearview mirror.

"I read all about it." I say. Ema is still staring at me. "Monarchs are becoming extinct and it's all because of GMO. There's a new study . . ."

"It's not new, and it's not true," Abba says. His eyes

are focused on the road. "The decline of the monarch butterflies and milkweed started well before the introduction of genetically modified crops. You really should read more than just one old article, Shai."

I should've known he would deny it.

"And it really has absolutely nothing to do with what I do."

"Well," I say, "people don't like scientists messing with their food either."

"People also don't like buying bruised apples . . ."

"What does that have to do with anything?"

"Take a left here," Ema says.

Abba goes on: "The non-browning apple that has just been approved—"

"Left, left!" Ema is all about giving directions. I wish we weren't going to the Levis'.

"I'm turning, Neta." He's turning, but he keeps talking as if he weren't interrupted. "By silencing one gene, we get an apple that doesn't brown. Up until recently, forty percent of apples were thrown away because people don't want to buy bruised apples."

"I think it's the house with the green door." Ema points.

"And people prefer buying their apples sliced."

"Can we continue this conversation later?" Ema says.

"No!" Gili jumps out of her seat. "It's boring."

"We will," Abba says and looks at me as he reverses to park.

Whatever. No point. I'll never be able to convince him that what he's doing is wrong.

* * *

It smells good at the Levi house. Almost like Friday night at Safta's. Lily Levi sets Ema's challah in the center of the table near the candles. But the Shabbat table will never look perfect without my grandparents.

Yael Levi takes me to her room to show me her pet hamster, but she won't let me hold it. She goes on and on about this Israeli TV show that she apparently watches online. I never liked that show very much, but I just nod as she updates me about the characters. I don't want to be impolite. She talks about them like they're real people she knows. She says watching the show helps her with her Hebrew.

I used to watch a lot of American TV shows back in Israel, but now I know I have to start talking, not just listening, for my English to really improve. I don't tell Yael that. Maybe her mom invited us over because she thought we would be good for her kids' Hebrew. But Yael's talking to me in English about this boring show. She was born here and prefers to speak English. I'm glad when Lily calls us downstairs for dinner.

Maybe I should go to Olivia's sleepover. I can probably still go after dinner. I like Olivia better than Yael.

Avi Levi says the kiddush, then passes the wine between the adults.

"So," he says after we sit down to eat, "glad to have you here with us in the great US of A."

I don't like the way he says this. It feels to me like he's trashing Israel.

"Cheers!" Lily raises a toast, and the other adults join.

"First time you go back to visit in Israel, you won't be able to imagine how you've ever lived there. Humid summers, crowded roads, rude customer service . . ."

"But we love it, right?" Abba says, but Avi takes a deep breath, getting ready to go on with his horror list.

I don't want to hear any more. "May I be excused to the bathroom?"

"Sure, dear," Lily says and points a long finger. "It's down the hall, first door to your left." Her expression is relieved, like she's glad I changed the subject.

But it doesn't do the trick. Avi is back on his rant before I reach the bathroom. I shut the door behind me. I hear the tone but not the words. Phew! Saved by the toilet.

Abba starts to say something, but Avi cuts him off. He's louder now, and he's talking about terrorism. I turn on the faucet and wash my hands twice as long as usual, drowning all the voices beyond the bathroom.

The coconutty hand soap shifts my attention from my ears to my nose. I wash my hands again. The towel is soft, and I keep holding it even after my hands are dry, realizing it's time to step back out there. Maybe I should tell Ema about the sleepover. Then we'll have a good excuse to leave.

"Dessert," Lily says as soon as I show up in the dining room. She gives Avi an *enough already* look.

He stops talking for a minute and pours himself a glass of Coke. When Lily goes into the kitchen to bring the dessert, he says, "Isn't it great that here, when you buy a drink at a restaurant, you can get as many refills as you want? That would never work in Israel. People would buy one drink and have all the family drink from refills." He probably does that. I saw him not return his cart at the market.

"I would say you are generalizing," Abba says.

Yes. Go Abba. For a second I forgive him for his GMO sins.

"Come on, Oren, you know Israelis," Avi says. "We take advantage of the system. I guess it's a cultural thing."

I knew it. He's one of those Israelis he's complaining about. Hypocrite.

"*We're* Israelis, and we don't do that," I say.

Lily comes back from the kitchen. "Chocolate cake and vanilla ice cream," she declares. A little too loudly.

"We should be extra careful to *not* do things like that," Ema says. "It is our responsibility to be good ambassadors of Israel."

I'm proud of my parents. At this point, they probably don't want to be here at the Levis' any more than I do. "I was invited to a sleepover tonight," I whisper to Ema.

Her eyes shine. "Why didn't you tell me?" she whispers back. "That's great. You should go."

After dessert, Ema says that we have to leave since I have to get to a party.

I'm kind of hoping that it's also because she is annoyed by Avi.

CHAPTER 12

SLEEPºVER, MAKEOVER, AND MEAN GIRLS

That's exactly what Olivia will look like thirty years from now, I think when her mom opens the door. Ema shakes her hand and thanks her for inviting me. *Tanks* her. She's never going to master the "th."

"I adore your accent," Olivia's mom says, giggling. The exact same giggle as Olivia's.

Olivia possibly has a mother who's even more embarrassing than mine.

Ema kisses me on the head and tells me to have fun. In Hebrew. Okay, she's still at the top of the Most Embarrassing Moms list.

The house is dim with lots of dark, heavy furniture. I can't even tell if there are windows behind the olive-green drapes. And everything is so organized it looks like no one lives here.

"So you're Shai," Olivia's mom says. "I wish she had updated me that you RSVP'd."

Aresveepeed? I stare at her, knowing I probably have the same expression on my face as Gili does when spoken to in English. I have no idea what she just said.

"It's okay. There's plenty of food," she says, smiling a little too big. "Olivia!" she yells up the staircase. "Surprise! Shai is here."

Plenty of food? Maybe she meant I didn't confirm that I'm coming? Nah, a sleepover wouldn't require the same formalities as a wedding or a bar mitzvah. Or maybe in America it does.

Olivia runs down the stairs. "Shai? You came! Come on up. Everyone else is already up in my room."

Is "everyone" Jenny and the M's? I should've guessed that. Maybe it wasn't the best idea to come here.

I follow Olivia down the dark corridor. More dark furniture.

Unlike the rest of the house, Olivia's room is super bright. Jenny and the M's are spread out on the lavender carpet. Everything is totally matching: the bedspread, the furniture, the curtains. Olivia throws herself on a giant fuzzy beanbag next to the bed.

"Hey, everybody, Shai's here," she says. She sounds different than she did when it was just the two of us in PE. Unnatural.

Jenny gets up to hug me.

"Let's do our nails," Mia says.

It *was* a mistake to come here.

"Yes." Madison jumps up. She takes a huge box from Olivia's closet. It has every possible color imaginable.

What I have in acrylic paint, she has in nail polish. And it's all organized in rainbow order.

"Shai," Madison says, "what color do you want? Pick one for your fingers and one for your toes. Maybe blue to match your eyes and your cast?"

"Ah. Umm. I'm not a big fan of nail polish." I put my hands behind my back. I want to offer to paint their nails, but I've never done it before. Nails are different than canvas or paper. Or casts or walls.

Mia is lying on her stomach on the carpet next to Madison, flipping through magazines. She opens to a page were the model has hair as long and dark as mine, except it's super straight. "I wonder how Shai would look with straight hair," she says.

"Olivia!" Jenny calls out. "Bring your flat iron and some of your mom's makeup. We're doing an extreme makeover on Shai."

"I like my hair the way it is," I say. "And my nails. And I don't wear makeup." I add, "Sorry. I'm really not into this sort of stuff."

"Is that an Israeli thing?" Jenny asks.

She should see my friends in Israel. Their extreme makeovers are way more extreme than hers. "No," I say. "It's totally a Shai thing." Ella, Tal, and Shir have given up on trying to talk me into makeup and nail polish and dresses.

"Can I at least braid your hair?" Olivia asks.

"Sure." I've said too many no's already. Even though it always hurts when someone else combs my hair, even Ema.

Olivia brushes my hair gently, getting all the tangles out. She's actually better at it than Ema, who's been doing the brushing and shampooing for me ever since I broke my arm. "Your hair is awesome. It's so thick," she says, "and so soft."

Madison is painting Jenny's nails while Olivia is braiding my hair.

"Maybe we could do each finger in a different color," Madison says.

"No way!" Jenny says. "Do you want me to look like Kay-Lee the Clown?"

They all laugh.

"Speaking of the clown girl . . . Shai, I've been meaning to tell you my big news. I got her spot in art. Starting Monday. Isn't that great? Thanks for the tip, Shy-Shai. Couldn't have done it without you."

Wow. She didn't.

"Are you mad at me?" she asks.

Olivia's eyeballs ping-pong between Jenny and me, but she doesn't say anything. I can tell she thinks it's wrong, and I wish she'd say something.

I shrug. My hand freezes on my neck. Oh no, oh no, oh no! My necklace is gone.

I look around me.

"Are you okay?" Jenny asks. "I didn't think you'd take it so hard. Sorry, Shy-Shai."

"It's fine." I'll be glad to have Kay-Lee instead of Jenny in band. But right now, I couldn't care less about this. This Star of David pendant has been in my family for probably a hundred years. How will I tell Ema? Maybe it's in her car. I just got here. I couldn't have lost it here. But maybe I did. I don't want to say anything. I don't feel like sleeping here anymore.

Olivia accidentally pulls my hair.

"Ouch."

"Oops. Sorry," Olivia says.

"Movie time," Jenny says. Like it's her party.

Olivia puts the brush down. At least my hair is thankful for Jenny's bossiness.

"I'll make us some popcorn, and we'll watch *Mean Girls*," Olivia says.

I've seen it in Israel at least ten times.

I'm glad we're done with the makeover part. I scan the carpet for my Star of David before Olivia dims the lights for the movie.

The popcorn is good, but my stomach hurts whenever I think about how these girls laughed about Kay-Lee.

Mean girls.

I reach for my Star of David and remember it's gone. I want to go home.

I tell Olivia I have a stomachache, which is true, and call Ema to come pick me up.

The necklace, the meanness, the makeup—all scrambling in my guts like popcorn in process.

Ema doesn't interrogate me in the car like I thought she would. She just says she's proud of me for trying, which is the perfect thing to say. And it proves she understands me if she makes an effort—that's why I get upset when she doesn't.

I turn around, hoping to see the glitter of my Star of David in the back seat. Ema gives me a questioning look. I almost tell her, but I'm afraid her reaction would ruin her understanding record, which is pretty perfect at the moment.

She holds out her hand, and I think she wants to give me a squeeze to substitute for the hug she'd probably give me if she wasn't driving. I start to reach over—and I see it, shining in the palm of her hand. I take it and stare at it until it's blurry. The clasp is broken, but it's okay otherwise.

"Lily Levi found it and called me. I drove back to pick it up."

"Thank you."

We drive in silence for a while. The radio isn't even on. There's just the sound of the blinker when Ema turns left or right. I want to ask Ema if she's happy here, if she's okay with sacrificing our life where we belong for a life where we don't, just for the sake of Abba's career. But I know she'll be on Abba's side, and I'm too tired to confront her. "Lily Levi is nice," I say to break the silence.

Ema nods. "She is. Did you like Yael? It would be great if you had an Israeli friend." She's assuming it was so bad at Olivia's that I'll never have American friends. Is it true?

"Yeah," I say. But really, I know that the fact that we're both Israelis isn't going to make us friends. I wouldn't be friends with her back in Israel, so why should I here? I wouldn't have been friends with Jenny and the M's back home either. Maybe Olivia. But did she have to laugh when they made fun of Kay-Lee?

CHAPTER 13

TRUMPETS, FLYER, AND FRIENDSHIP

I wake up to almost no stomachache, just a little trace of the sleepover-gone-bad. I decide not to think about it on the weekend, but sometimes when I decide not to think about something, the "something" keeps popping up in my brain. The trick is to find a new something to think about.

My grandparents are coming tomorrow. Good one.

My necklace is on the nightstand, all fixed. Ema must have done that after I went to bed. I put it back on. Saba and Safta will be happy to see I'm still wearing it.

The doorbell rings. It's Kay-Lee—wearing a flowery, vintage-looking dress, a '50s or '60s or some-decade-that's-not-the-one-we-live-in type of dress that not everybody can pull off, but she does. She has lots of thin bracelets in matching colors on her wrist. And silver flip flops.

"Hi, Shai," she says, smiling not only with her mouth but also with her eyes. "I came to check on

Zoe. She usually doesn't get out of the house much."
I didn't even realize she was here.

Ema shows up behind me. "She's outside in the pool with Gili. She's welcome to stay, and so are you. Show Kay-Lee de wall painting you did, Shai."

It's called a mural, I want to say. But I don't. Don't want to embarrass her like she's embarrassing me. She doesn't mean to. But really, it's not just how she speaks, it's what she says. Now I'll have to take Kay-Lee up to my room, and it's a mess.

"Gili and I painted a mural in my room," I say.

"I'd love to see it," Kay-Lee says. Sounds like she really does.

"Yofi! Bo-ee ee-tee . . ." Oh no, I didn't just do that. "Sorry. I meant, 'Good. Come with me.'" Ugh, I'm more embarrassing than Ema.

Kay-Lee follows me up the stairs. "Was that Hebrew?" she asks.

"Sorry," I say. I'll die if that happens to me at school.

"It's cool," Kay-Lee says.

I lead her to my room, hoping there is no dirty underwear on the floor. "Try to look only at the wall," I say.

"Don't worry about it. My room is always a total mess," she says as we go in. "Wow!"

"Does that mean my room is wow-messier than yours?" I ask. But I notice her eyes are on the wall.

"No. The mural is incredible. You're so talented—I absolutely love it." She walks over and taps a finger against it, like she's checking if it's dry. Next, she strokes it with her whole hand. "I wish I could draw like that. I sew," she says, gesturing with both hands on the sides of her dress, "but I can't draw."

"I did it after I heard I couldn't choose art as my elective," I say, "and hey, I heard you decided to switch to band."

"How did you know?"

I tell her how Jenny bragged about getting her spot in art.

Her eyes open wide, then shrink until they're almost shut, then reopen with a slight hint of *I'm not going to say what I wanted to say.* She's not the gossiping type—I like that about her.

"What instrument do you play?" she asks.

"Trumpet," I say. "Mr. Belton says it's the easiest to start with. You'll like him."

"Hey, ChrisFacts plays the trumpet. I mean Chris Harris." Kay-Lee dangles her bracelets. "Do you know him?"

"I think so." I try to sound casual. "There is a Chris who plays the trumpet. He's also in my math class."

"By the look on your face, we're talking about the same one. Ahhh, ChrisFacts—another good reason to be in band." She pronounces "Chris" and "facts" as if it's one long word.

"I probably should go check on Zoe," she says, and we both go downstairs.

Gili and Zoe are splashing each other. Gili makes enough noise for both of them.

We sit on the side of the pool and put our feet in the water. Kay-Lee has neon-orange nail polish on her toenails. I hate nail polish, but it looks good on her.

"Looks like Zoe will be learning some Hebrew," Kay-Lee says.

"My parents were hoping it would be the other way around."

"Yeah, it takes some getting used to—the fact that she doesn't speak. Ever since . . ." She stops mid-sentence and sighs. She takes off her bracelets and switches them to her other wrist. Maybe she's not aware that she's doing it, kind of like me with my Star of David. I don't say anything. Whatever she was going to say, she obviously decided not to. Does it have to do with her mom leaving? Should I even trust the gossipy M's?

She stirs the water in circular motion with her orange toes.

"Why do you call Chris ChrisFacts?" I ask to switch the subject—but also because I really want to know.

She takes her bracelets off and puts them on the opposite wrist. "He's just so into facts. And not just plain boring facts. Usually it's weird, random, but kind of interesting stuff that no one else would know, like 'Did you know'"—she switches into a deeper voice trying to imitate him—"'that in Italy you have to pay for McDonald's ketchup and mayonnaise packets?'"

I laugh. "He's been telling me facts about Israel every chance he gets."

"That sounds like him," Kay-Lee says. "With me it's always about color, which is kind of cute. It got me researching it myself—so I can answer. Like he'd say, 'Blue is the color of loyalty and trust,' and I'd say, 'But American culture evolved it into a symbol of depression.'"

"Really?" I ask. "Blue is my favorite color. Is it really a symbol of depression?"

"Yeah. You know how people say 'feeling blue' when they're sad?"

"I never heard that. That doesn't exist in Hebrew," I say.

"Interesting how every language has its own idioms," Kay-Lee says. "Anyway, last year Chris got obsessed with facts from around the world. Oh!" Kay-Lee slaps her forehead. "Around the world." She splashes water with her feet in a circular motion. "There's this World Peace drawing competition. You don't have to be in art to enter. It's open to every student in America." Now she's tapping the butterflies on my cast. "I bet you could win it. Come on over to my house. I'll give you the flyer with all the details."

Flyer. Sounds like a word to describe someone who flies. I imagine her handing me a little winged creature who sings out competition announcements.

"Ema!" I yell. "I'm going over to Kay-Lee's." I'm more excited about going to Kay-Lee's than I am about the drawing competition.

It feels like friendship.

CHAPTER 14

CRANES, SNEAKERS, AND POODLES

"Dad, this is the not-so-shy Shai I was telling you about."
Kay-Lee introduces me to her father. "Zoe is having
fun at their house."

Kay-Lee's dad shakes my hand, quick and strong,
but his hand is warm and so is his smile. "We are so
happy to have you and your family next door. Zoe
stopped talking when her mom left . . ."

I look at Kay-Lee. Her eyes grow wide, like she's
wishing she could swallow her dad's words with
a look.

But he goes on. "My mother has been reading with
her and trying different exercises to get her to speak."
He pauses and sighs. "With your sister, she seems to
communicate perfectly without language."

I force a smile.

Kay-Lee grabs my hand. "Come on. I'll show you
my room."

Their house has the same ugly beige carpet as
ours does. Upstairs, the walls are lined with rows of

black-and-white pictures, like little windows with a view to the past. I want to stop and look at them all, but I have to keep up with Kay-Lee, who's walking fast down the hallway.

Kay-Lee's room is even more colorful than I imagined. Not the straight-from-a-magazine colorfulness like Olivia's, definitely not boring like Yael's. There's a table with a sewing machine, and above it, covering most of the wall, is a wooden pegboard holding every possible kind of sewing equipment. On the wall across from her bed, up on a high shelf, there's a row of probably fifty paper cranes. They all have a pattern on them that looks like tiny handwriting. Cranes made of letters.

Kay-Lee shoves a bunch of clothes under her bed and quickly straightens up the covers. "See?" she says. "I told you my room is messier than yours."

Her bed cover is a patchwork of probably over a hundred different fabric scraps. "Did you sew that yourself?" I ask.

"Yep."

"That's amazing," I say. "Much more impressive than fish painted on a wall."

"I'll sew you a dress if you paint me a mural."

Is she serious? I think she is. I almost say I don't wear dresses, but that would be rude. I look around. "A black-and-white mural would look great in here."

"Black and white isn't really my thing," she says, making a face I don't know how to interpret. "Anyway, first you have a competition to focus on." She grabs a pile of papers from her desk and flips through them. "Here it is," she says and hands me a piece of paper.

CHILDREN FOR PEACE, it says in bold letters at the top. I scan through parts of the text. *Imagine a peaceful world . . . Calling all creative teens. Students in grades 5–12 . . . Registration is free . . . Any medium may be used . . . No 3D entries . . . All entries must convey the theme of the competition . . .*

"I would enter it, but I can't draw half as well as you," Kay-Lee says, "and I can't think of anything original. It's all been done before—different nationalities and skin colors circling the globe, holding hands. I can't think of anything that isn't cheesy."

What does cheese have to do with it? Either she's awfully weird, or it's another expression that I don't get.

My eyes wander across the room. There is a touch of black and white in here: the paper cranes.

Kay-Lee notices I'm staring at them. "Those are letters from my mom," she mumbles almost to herself.

I feel my eyes widening Gili-fish style. "Oh."

"Come on." Kay-Lee jumps up from the bed. "Let's go make some OMG cookies."

Oh. The sneaker-poodles she's so proud of. They're non-GMO. I try to fake a smile.

"Snickerdoodles," she says, all cheery.

"Why do they have this weird name? Snea? Ker . . ." I try slowly.

Kay-Lee starts laughing and lands back on the bed. "*Snicker*, not *sneaker*, silly," she says.

"Oh." There's a tiny difference, one that I wouldn't be able to repeat. It's an accent thing. I laugh too. "I thought the cookies were named after shoes." I pause. "And poodles."

"I love that! That's even better than OMG cookies. Don't tell Gili." Kay-Lee smiles. "You're right—it is a strange name for cookies. I never thought to wonder why they're called that. They're Zoe's favorite cookies, and we always make them at home since my dad doesn't sell them at our family bakery. At the bakery, everything is French. The walls are covered with pictures from old black-and-white French films. Anyway, snickerdoodles aren't French, for sure."

She grabs me by the hand and pulls me out of her room. "Come on. Let's go bake some sneaker-poodles." She laughs all the way down to the kitchen.

The French bakery is probably all non-GMO too. She won't be laughing when she finds out what Abba does.

CHAPTER 15

DANGLING PARROTS, BLUE FOIL STARS, AND BLUE BUBBLEGUM TOOTHPASTE

Ema leaves early to pick Saba and Safta up from the airport.

I grab two pieces of paper from the printer and tape them together. I flip it so the tape is in the back, but you can still see the line that goes down the middle. I wish I had a bigger sheet. I write *Bruchim Ha'baeem Saba ve Safta* in chubby Hebrew letters. I fill in the letters with oil pastels. I use a different pattern in each one, kind of like Kay-Lee's quilt.

As I hang the sign on the front door, Zoe zips by on her scooter. Kay-Lee did say she's been getting out of the house more since she started coming over to our house. She stops next to me and stares at the sign.

"It says 'Welcome, Grandpa and Grandma,'" I explain. "*Saba* means grandpa, and *Safta* means grandma. Do you want to try and say it? It's easy. *Sa-ba, Sav-ta.*"

She shakes her head no. I wish I could get her to talk.

"Let me know if you ever want to try. New languages are hard, but they can also be fun." That probably didn't sound too convincing. She gives me a thumbs up and glides away.

I didn't lie. New languages are fun—if you don't need to actually use them instead of your first language to be understood.

I rush upstairs and shove all the clothes from the floor into the closet. I want my room to look nice when I show it to Saba and Safta. When I hear the car in our driveway, I run downstairs.

Safta comes out of the car first. Tan skin, snow-white hair, colorful outfit. My familiar Safta, just the way I love her. I jump into her arms. The plastic parrots in her giant hoop earrings rub against my shoulders as she hugs me tight. We're almost the same height.

I breathe in her familiar smell, and it lifts my heart like a hot-air balloon.

"You broke your arm, binti?" she says and gives Ema a look that says *hiding things from me, huh?*

"I didn't want to worry you," Ema says.

Safta looks back at me. "Beautiful artwork on that cast. Look what your talented granddaughter did, honey," she says to Saba, who comes from the other side of the car. He comes around and gives me one of his squishing hugs, letting all my hot air out. I forgot that his hugs hurt a little. I don't say anything. I just hope he doesn't break my other arm.

He takes a step back. "Let me take a look at my most beautiful granddaughter."

"Hey!" Gili jumps out of the car.

"Excuse me, Ms. Gili." He ruffles her hair. "I stand corrected: one of my two most beautiful granddaughters."

"One of four." I stand up for my twin cousins.

"Well, you two are the prettiest, and don't tell the other two I said that. If you do, I'll deny the whole thing." He winks at me and enters the house. "Hello?" his voice vibrates from the doorway. Abba comes downstairs to greet them. The parrots on Safta's earrings end up under his armpits when he gives her a hug.

For the first time, this house feels like home.

"We brought a few things." Safta points to her suitcase.

"Settle in first, Ema," my mother says to hers, and she shows her parents to the guest room.

Gili and I follow. Safta opens the suitcase and takes out everything she brought. When I see the domes of shiny blue foil in the see-through box, I can't believe my eyes.

"Krembo!" Gili and I scream at the same time.

Safta smiles and hands the box to Gili. I would've expected them to get all squished in the suitcase, but they look perfect. They survived the move to America better than I did.

Gili unwraps one, slowly and carefully to avoid tearing the thin foil. She shoves the Krembo in her mouth and runs to Saba with the wrapping.

There's a knock on the door. It's Zoe holding Motek's ball.

"How nice of you, Zoe," Ema says. "Come in and meet my parents."

"Krembo, Krembo! We got Krembo." Gili runs towards Zoe with half a Krembo in one hand and a shiny blue star that Saba just folded in the other.

"Tell Zoe what Krembo is," Gili says in Hebrew, twirling around Zoe.

"It's chocolate-coated with vanilla fluffy marshmallow-ish filling," I say, "and a sweet biscuit base on the bottom. But some people start eating it from the biscuit. In that case, the biscuit would be the top." Gosh, it's hard to explain Krembo. "Do you want to try one?"

Zoe nods a shy *yes*.

Ema gives her two. "One for Kay-Lee," she says.

"Now there'll be less for us," Gili complains. Good thing Zoe doesn't understand Hebrew.

Zoe curtsies a polite thank-you and leaves with two valuable Krembos.

"We should've told her to keep the wrapping for Saba's stars," Gili says.

Safta keeps pulling out stuff from her suitcase. "Shai." She hands me my favorite blue bubblegum-flavored toothpaste.

"You think there's no toothpaste in America?" Ema teases Safta. "Just every possible brand and flavor. And much cheaper too. You didn't have to carry this."

"My granddaughter asked for it," Safta says, "so I got her some." The parrots on her earrings sway as she shakes her head.

Ema looks at me.

"I wrote to her," I say. "I hate every single toothpaste you've bought here."

"Okay," Ema says. "It's between the two of you." Sounds like she's insulted.

Safta takes out our favorite chocolate spread, Israeli couscous, and lots of Israeli chocolate bars.

"You really didn't need to schlepp all this food with you," Ema says. "My friend Lily gets a lot of Israeli stuff at the international market. We just haven't gotten around to checking it out yet."

Safta goes on and unpacks the rest of their suitcases. She gives us letters and drawings from our cousins. "I hope these are okay," she says to Ema a little sarcastically.

Abba pops his head into the guest room. "You should rest for an hour or so," he says. "Then we can show you around."

Saba and Safta agree to take a short nap.

"When you miss someone, you only remember the good things about them," Ema mumbles to herself, but I hear it. I wish she'd appreciate Safta more.

CHAPTER 16

PILLOW FIGHT, FOLDING TRIANGLES, AND STAR OF DAVID

I wish I could talk to Ella, or Tal, or Shir, but it's past midnight in Israel.

I stare at the fish on my mural. They stare back. I stick my tongue out at them—I'm losing my mind. I get up and make faces at myself in the mirror.

I smell Safta entering my room. A moment later, I see her smiling in the mirror behind me. "What a beautiful job you did on this wall."

This is my chance to ask. I don't turn to face her. I look in her eyes through the mirror. "I can't stay here. I don't belong here," I say.

Safta sighs.

I turn around. "Can I go back to Israel with you and Saba? Please?"

"Binti, my love . . ." Safta sighs again. Bad sign.

"Pleeease." Can't she see I'm a squished Krembo? "I won't be any trouble. I can walk to school. And I'll help you around the house. I promise."

"Oh, Shai." She sits on my bed and taps her purple

fingernails on the bedsheets, inviting me to sit next to her. I do. She strokes my forehead, clearing the bangs from my eyes.

"When I was a kid, I left Iraq with my parents and moved to Israel. I wished more than anything else to stay with my grandparents in Baghdad."

"It's not the same," I say.

"You're right. The circumstances were very different. But what I'm saying is that Iraq was my home, and I didn't want to leave. I was nine years old. Old enough to understand that there was no future for the Jews in Iraq. The hatred was unbearable, and Israel was painted to us as the wonderful land of milk and honey, the place where we belong, but I felt like I belonged in Baghdad."

"But that's just it! Israel still *is* the place we belong!" I don't mean to yell at Safta, but I lose control of my own volume.

"All I'm saying is that I also felt a strong sense of belonging to the place where I was born and raised, and it took me some time to feel at home in a new place. But eventually I did. A child belongs where her family is."

"Well, your parents had no choice. They took you away for your safety, not for their career." I'm controlling my volume now, but not my tears.

Safta strokes my hair. "Sometimes life makes choices for you that you wouldn't make yourself, but they turn out to be right for you."

She doesn't get it. She thinks she does, but she really doesn't.

Safta pulls me closer to her, and I can smell her Safta-ness. It's a scent that is deep and sweet and reminds me of mango with a touch of something unique that grows only on our family tree.

It's the smell of home.

Safta wipes my tears and then rubs her hand up and down my arm like she's trying to keep me warm. "Come on, binti, let's go make my famous bourekas. I'll add an extra pinch of my magical cheering-up ingredient."

I fake a smile for her.

"Just so you know, it's hard to turn down your request to come live with us. We miss you all so much."

I put my head in her lap and cry.

Gili barges into the room. "Safta, aren't we making bourekas?"

I get up from Safta's lap, trying to cover my eyes so Gili won't see my tears.

"Pillow fight!" Safta yells and throws a pillow in my face.

I love my safta.

"Me too!" Gili says, picking up a pillow, throwing it at Safta.

Safta catches it and wraps it behind Gili's back, kissing her nose. "We'll be right down," she tells her.

"Can you go wake up Saba? If he sleeps all day, he'll never get over his jet lag."

When Gili leaves the room, Safta turns back to me. "Focus on the good. Sometimes it's not easy to find the good in bad situations, but do your best to find it. And focus on it."

I focus on her deep, blue eyes and promise to try.

* * *

Gili pulls up a chair and places it right beside Safta, as close as she can to the kitchen counter. Safta lines up the ingredients for the dough. I grate the mozzarella and mix it with the feta for the filling.

"Where's the mixer?" Safta asks.

"I don't have kitchen appliances that work here." Ema's voice cracks. "The voltage is different here, the measurements are different, everything's different— weight, temperature, distance. I don't know if I'll ever get used to it."

So let's just go back to Israel, I want to scream, but the words stay locked inside me.

"Of course you'll get used to it," Safta says. "People get used to worse things in life."

Ema turns to the sink and starts washing dishes, making way more noise that she usually does.

"We'll knead the dough the old-fashioned way."

Safta says, "I'm sure the bourekas will taste the same. Maybe even better."

Ema keeps clinking the dishes a little too loudly.

"Can you set the oven to 180, Shai?" Safta asks like nothing happened. She puts all the ingredients in a bowl and lifts Gili's hair into a ponytail. They both dig in their hands and start working.

"You're talking Celsius," Ema says. "Go figure Fahrenheit . . ."

It really shouldn't be such a big deal. I grab my phone and Google *Celsius to Fahrenheit*. "It's 356," I say and set the oven.

Gili and Safta flatten the dough and cut it into squares. Gili is unusually quiet. Maybe Ema's outburst scared her.

I put a spoonful of the cheese mix in the center of each square, and Gili and I both fold the squares into triangles, pinching the bourekas into shape. It reminds me of Saturdays at Safta's house, making bourekas with Aunt Sigal's twins.

In Israel, you can buy bourekas in every bakery, but Safta's are the best.

Safta walks over to the sink and stands closer to Ema.

"Focus on the good," I whisper as I fold triangles. Safta smiles at me from the other end of the kitchen.

Gili and I arrange the triangles on the oven tray and go sit by the pool. Gili jumps in the water. Motek jumps in right after her. I can't wait to get rid of this cast.

Through the glass door, I see Ema talking to Safta in the kitchen. I hope Ema's saying she wants to go back to Israel.

* * *

"The bourekas are ready," Safta calls. I go inside.

"You're already baking, Aviva?" Saba is finally up. He gives Safta a hug like he hasn't seen her in weeks. "Look at our beautiful granddaughter," he tells Safta. Gili is outside in the pool, so I guess he means me. I smile. Saba's eyes drift to my necklace. "You don't wear that to school, do you?" he asks.

"I wear it all the time," I say. "I never take it off."

Saba looks at Ema. "Not a good idea," he whispers.

Ema looks annoyed. "It's not an idea, Abba. It's a necklace that's been on her neck since you two gave it to her. It reminds her of you. Why should she not wear it? We're not in Nazi Germany."

Saba just stares at her. Ema stares back. Safta looks back and forth from Saba to Ema, but she doesn't say anything.

Saba clears his throat. I touch my necklace.

"Not. Everybody. Likes. Jews," Saba says in a low and slow voice that really scares me.

Gili walks in all wet from the pool. "Why?" she asks.

"Seriously, Abba?" Ema tilts her head in Gili's way. "Gili, please go change out of that wet bathing suit right now."

Surprisingly, Gili goes upstairs without arguing.

"This is southern California. Diverse and liberal. Please don't put any paranoid thoughts in my daughters' heads." Ema sounds mad. Not the same kind of mad as earlier with the Celsius and Fahrenheit—much scarier.

"Your dad might have a point, Neta," Safta says.

"Not you too," Ema says.

"I still remember the boy who called me a stinky Jew and spit on me," Safta says.

"Ema, we're not in Iraq. This is America. And it's the twenty-first century."

"Somebody really spit on you, Safta?" I ask. "What did you do?"

"I spit right back in his face. But after that, my mom never let me go play outside until we moved to Israel."

I cling to the Star of David, sliding it from side to side along its chain.

"I smell Safta Aviva's bourekas!" Abba walks in after a run, oblivious to the drama. He snatches a bourekas right off the hot tray. "Mmmmm, we missed your baking, Aviva."

Gili runs downstairs.

"Should we take Saba and Safta to the beach?" Abba looks at Gili.

"Yes!" Gili jumps up and down. "I'll bring my Dora the Explorer boogie board."

"Sounds nice," Safta says. Everything sounds nice to her.

"I don't like the beach here," I say.

Abba almost chokes on the bourekas. "People come to the beaches of southern California from all over the world. Tourists, journalists, surfers."

We went to the beach when we first got here a month ago, but the water was freezing. Abba said it's because the Pacific Ocean is so much bigger than the Mediterranean. Also, the sand here is not as soft. I don't care what tourists from around the world think. I miss my small, warm ocean. The beach is so much more fun in Tel Aviv. Here, there's no gazlan yelling, "Chocolate, banana, lemon, pineapple!" There probably isn't even a word for *gazlan* in English, because there isn't such a person here who walks around at the beach, carrying a cooler on his back, selling all these flavors of popsicles.

"There are squirrels at the beach here!" Gili says.

"Squirrels are just overrated mice with disproportionate tails," I say.

"Well, it's too late for a bigger adventure." Abba grabs another bourekas. "We'll take Saba and Safta for a walk on the beach. Whoever wants to join is welcome."

"Maybe you shouldn't wear your necklace to the beach, Shai," Safta says.

Ema gives her a look.

"I don't want her to lose it, that's all," Safta says.

"It's fine," I say, holding myself back from telling her I did almost lose it a few days ago.

"Let's go find our bathing suits," Safta says to Saba. "I hope I remembered to pack them."

I go upstairs to change. I manage to take my necklace off, despite the cast.

I check that the clasp closes tightly, so I won't lose it at the beach. And I put it back on.

CHAPTER 17

FIRST PLACE, FRUIT COLORS, AND CHERRY TOMATOES

I easily spot Kay-Lee at lunch. She's wearing a fruit-patterned, Hawaiian-looking dress.

"You forgot this at my house," she says, handing me the flyer for the drawing competition.

I read through it again. This time I read all of it. "First prize is a flight to any place around the world?" I can't believe this. This is my chance. If I win this, I'm out of here. "Any place I choose?" I must have said that too loud. Heads turn in our direction.

Kay-Lee laughs her wind-chime laughter. "Yes, silly, but don't go packing your suitcase just yet. You have to win first."

I'm speed-planning this new idea in my head. I can win this. I'll call my parents right before I board the plane, so they won't be worried that I've disappeared. I'll call Safta to come pick me up when I land in Israel. She might be a little mad at first, but once she realizes how serious I am about coming back and sees that I did it all on my own, she'll let me stay. She'll realize she should have agreed to take me back in the first place.

I fold the flyer carefully and tuck it in my bag. This is my ticket back home. This plan has to work.

Pat and Matt walk by. Pat points at us. "Aww, look," he says to Matt. "The color creep is having lunch with the new Jew."

They keep walking, laughing like Pat told the funniest joke ever.

"Ignore them," Kay-Lee says. Exactly what Olivia said at PE.

My stomach feels wobbly. I slide the Star of David on my necklace from side to side, aware that I'm doing it this time. Maybe Saba was right. Maybe I should take it off.

* * *

Jenny bumps into me on the way to language arts. "Where were you at lunch?" she asks in an accusing tone. "Everybody was asking about you."

I tell her I had lunch with Kay-Lee, and her eyes roll up as if she's trying to take a look at her own brain. "Well, I won't see you in band today. Wish me luck in art," she says. "I guess I'll see you tomorrow morning in history."

"Good luck." And good riddance.

Nurse Sweetie is actually pretty sweet. I sit in her office during my PE period and do my homework to the background sounds of the sick and the injured. Not only does she call everybody sweetie, she also hands out sweets.

On my way to band, I see Kay-Lee, and we walk together.

Mr. Belton is standing at the door like always. "Hello, Shy Butterfly. I see you brought a friend with you."

Kay-Lee introduces herself and reaches her hand out to shake Mr. Belton's.

He smiles like you would at a little kid who just did something super adult and shakes Kay-Lee's hand. "Definitely the hand of a flutist," he says, "and you are in luck, my friend. We have one loaner flute still left in the storage room, and now I know with certainty it was waiting for you."

Chris is in the storage room putting his trumpet together. He looks up at Kay-Lee. "Look who joined band," he says. "Red is dominant today. Ahhhh, the color of love."

Kay-Lee doesn't blush as easily as I do. "It can also be the color of war, blood, and danger, you know," she tells him.

"So which is it?" Chris asks. The flirting is definitely mutual.

"Be careful," Kay-Lee says. "I haven't decided yet."

"Do you have a vegetable dress too?" a boy cleaning his tuba says.

How does she stand these comments? She probably hears them all day, but she still dresses the way she does.

"I have a tomato T-shirt," Kay-Lee says. I'm not sure if she's being serious or not, but it sounds like a good answer and it shuts this kid up. He's deep-cleaning his tuba, pretending he didn't hear her.

"Cherry tomatoes!" Chris jumps and points to me. "Those were created in Israel."

I give Kay-Lee a questioning look.

"If Chris says so, then it's true," she says.

One thing is true for sure: She has a much bigger crush on him than I do.

CHAPTER 18

CHOCOLATE MOUSSE CAKE, JESUS KILLER, AND DANCING QUEEN

Safta makes tbeet, kibbeh, kebab, and a huge, round challah. "You have to eat round things on the evening of Rosh Hashanah," she says. "It symbolizes the circle of life. One year ends; a new one begins."

She arranges apple slices in the shape of a flower, with a little bowl of honey in the center, for a sweet new year. Ema wanted to invite the Levis, but they've gone to Israel. We don't know anyone else around here who celebrates the Jewish holidays.

It's a regular day to everyone else. At least it falls on a Saturday this year. Would I have gone to school if it were on a weekday? If I didn't, I'd have to make up everything I missed.

I hate that you don't feel the holiday all around. Having a private holiday is like laughing alone at a joke that nobody else gets.

Ema set the table with a white tablecloth, white flowers, and Shabbat candles—because it's a holiday—and blue helium balloons tied to each chair.

Because it's my birthday.

I usually celebrate twice, going by both the Jewish calendar and the modern one. The two calendars match up only every nineteen years. But this year I don't feel like celebrating at all. A private holiday plus a birthday without my friends adds up to double-depressing day.

I thought that even my best friends in Israel wouldn't remember it's my birthday—we haven't talked much lately. But Ella called this morning. It was evening there, so they were on the way to her grandmother's house in Haifa, stuck in holiday traffic. "Happy birthday and happy holiday! Love you, miss you, hug-hug-kiss you," she said in English before we hung up. It made me cry just a little. I'm not sure why.

Saba says the holiday prayer. He does it so much better than Abba.

"L'chaim!" Everybody puts forward their wine glass, raising a toast.

Gili and I have tirosh, which is grape juice, but we call it kids' wine. Ema found it at a regular grocery store in the kosher section.

Saba makes a toast for my thirteenth birthday. It's been a year since my bat mitzvah.

"If you were American, you'd have your bat mitzvah now," Abba says. I don't know why some Jewish girls celebrate at thirteen here, like boys.

"I'm not American," I say. And that concludes this conversation.

"Can you pass the tomato salad?" Abba points at the salad bowl, asking no one in particular.

"Were cherry tomatoes invented in Israel?" I ask.

"Yes." Saba sits taller. "Two professors at the Jerusalem Hebrew University developed the first version of cherry tomatoes. Your dad would know more about it." So Chris was right.

Abba sits up straighter too, as if there's a let's-sit-up-straight-and-set-the-record-straight competition going on. "I'm glad you brought that up."

"Is that kind of similar to what you're doing with the avocados, Oren?" Safta asks.

"Sort of, but what we're doing is considered GMO—genetic modification. Growing cherry tomatoes is considered crossbreeding."

"What's the difference?" Safta asks.

"Crossbreeding is creating a hybrid between two different species. It's done with less precision than the lab-controlled GMO we do. And it's not tested since it's traditional—and therefore automatically considered safe. GMO foods, on the other hand, have to go through years and years of testing before being released to the market. They've been proven safe, but people sometimes focus on the mistakes made by a few greedy corporations instead of the careful research being done by scientists."

He's talking about his work again. On my birthday. Unbelievable. Can't he stop thinking about his job for this one day? Worst birthday ever. I want to leave the table, but Ema comes from the kitchen with a big pot, announcing, "Kreplach soup!"

I'll tolerate any conversation topic for kreplach soup.

"I'm so happy for you that you're getting your cast removed on Monday, Shai," Safta says, changing the topic. Love my safta. "Can I come along? I'd love to see that Dr. Seuss office."

I look at Ema. "Sure," she says.

At least the kreplach don't disappoint—they taste like holiday-and-birthday put together. Ema learned how to make them from my other safta, the one I never got to meet.

Safta made her famous three-layered chocolate mousse especially for my birthday. The top layer is white chocolate, my favorite. Saba would normally make some remark about it being dairy after meat, but he doesn't. The rest of the family doesn't care too much that it isn't kosher.

Safta lights the candles on the cake and tells me to make a wish.

I wish that Safta and Saba won't leave, and I blow

out the candles knowing it won't come true. So I tell myself to focus on the good, remembering to simply be glad that they're here on my birthday.

* * *

I start the week with focusing on the good. I hate having history first period, but the good thing is that I'm done with it first thing in the morning.

"Today we're going to start a chapter about the ancient Israelites," Mr. Ford says.

Half the heads in class turn my way. I don't know most of these kids. How do they even know I'm from Israel? Mr. Ford doesn't notice. He flips through the pages of the history book on his desk. "Open the book to page ninety-three, please."

"The Jews killed Jesus," someone whispers in the back. Heads turn again. Now it feels like every pair of eyes in the classroom is focused on me.

My stomach seems to be searching for a better space within me. Not sure I'll be able to keep up the focusing-on-the-good strategy.

"What's all the commotion?" Mr. Ford asks. The class goes quiet. "Please read the chapter quietly," he says.

"You should really take that Star of David off," Jenny whispers to me, sounding like Saba. "I'm Jewish too, you know, but I don't put it on display for everyone to comment on."

I didn't know she's Jewish. I cling to the Star of David on my neck.

Focus on the good. Safta's voice is in my head. I look down at my cast. I'm getting it off today.

It's my last day going to Nurse Sweetie. The "Nurse's Office" sign on her door is old and faded, so I decide to make her a new one. I draw the letters to look like bandages, pills, and syringes, and I draw rows of candy around the edges framing it all. Drawing clears my mind of bad thoughts. I draw tiny drops of blood next to the syringes as I try to shake away the memory of this morning's history class.

Nurse Sweetie hangs the sign right away. She hugs me and tells me how much she loves it. "I will miss you, Shai-sweetie. Please be well but come and visit me at my office from time to time."

I promise to do that. I slide the Star of the David on my necklace throughout the whole day, finally letting go of it when it's time to hold my trumpet.

The band room is the only part of this school that I like. The three-legged metal music stands are all lined up, their upper parts at just the right angle, waiting to support the music sheets. Something about that neat row soothes me.

Kay-Lee walks in right after me.

"Hello, Kaleidoscope Kay-Lee," Mr. Belton says.

Kay-Lee smiles. Mr. Belton's the best. I'm glad there was no room in art. Maybe this is what Safta meant by "life choosing for you."

* * *

Safta waves to me from the passenger seat next to Ema as I approach the car.

I get in the back seat. Safta's favorite group is playing on the radio. It's an old Swedish band called ABBA, for the initials of the band members' names. They probably have no idea it means *father* in Hebrew. I wish their initials were SAFTA. The two that have a name starting with a B would just have to change their names to start with F and T. Then they'd need a fifth member whose name starts with S. I'd take the job, but I'm not too good at singing, and I wouldn't want to move to Sweden anyway.

Safta turns up the volume. Ema and Safta sing along to the lyrics about the sweet, seventeen-year-old dancing queen.

"I remember when this song was released," Safta says. "Saba used to say that I wasn't as young, but I was twice as sweet." She says that every time we hear this song, but I don't mind hearing this story for the thousandth time.

* * *

At the Lorax's office, Safta walks around like it's a museum until the nurse calls us in.

I close my eyes so I don't have to watch the saw go through the butterflies. Dr. Lorax is very pleased with the healing. But without the cast I feel heavier, not lighter. My arm feels tingly and looks pale, and I miss my blue butterflies already.

CHAPTER 19

NUTTY PATTY, COCKROACHES, AND SATAN'S DAY OFF

Mrs. Adams says we'll be working in groups building a DNA model. Abba would love it, but I won't give him the pleasure of knowing about this project. He would want to help for sure, but I don't want his help. The Jews-killed-Jesus embarrassment reminded me that I should still be mad at him for moving us here.

Mrs. Adams had us move seats to sit next to our partners. I'm with Jenny, Chris, and Hakim.

"No more butterflies, huh?" Chris says. Can he tell there are butterflies in my stomach?

"Did you see her awesome cast before?" he asks Hakim. Oh, he means the cast.

Hakim shrugs. He hates me. How are we going to do this project together?

Jenny leans in super close to me. She points a finger in Hakim's direction, covering it with the palm of her other hand. "She really put *us* in a group with *him*?"

"What?" I say, a little too loudly. Mrs. Adams shushes me. "What did you just say?" This time

I whisper and stare at Jenny.

She puts on a *what did I do wrong?* expression. I want to kick her under the table.

"I had a sample model here somewhere." Mrs. Adams is rummaging through her messy closet. "Where could I have put it?" She's talking to herself, then to us. "Start discussing your project. You can plan to make the model out of anything you want. I'll be right back."

As soon as she's out the door, Pat turns around to face Chris. "So you're partnered with the Jew and the terrorist."

What is wrong with these kids?

"Shut up," Chris says with his mouth barely open, like he's trying to control himself.

"Such a jerk," the girl sitting next to him says. "Just because the guy is from Iraq doesn't make him a terrorist."

"I should punch him in the face," Chris says, "but Mrs. Adams should be back any minute."

"Did you hear that?" Pat elbows Hakim. "Your bodyguard here wants to punch me. You probably trained him, terrorist."

Jenny laughs.

"Do you really think that's funny?" I snap. Jenny chokes her laughter with a fake cough and rushes to the sign-out sheet next to the door, excusing herself to go to the bathroom.

My mind is on fire. I stare at Pat. "If he's a terrorist, then you're . . . allergic to peanuts!" Did I really just say that?

"What?" Pat stares at me.

So does Chris.

"It's the first silly generalization I could think of about Americans." I whisper to him.

"Yeah!" Chris calls. "She's right, Nutty Patty."

"Found it!" Mrs. Adams comes back with a plastic DNA helix in her hands.

My face is burning up. Nutty Patty turns away from us. Did he get it? Calling someone a terrorist just because he's Muslim is as ridiculous as saying he's allergic to peanuts just because he's American, I explain to him. In my mind.

Mrs. Adams goes over the different parts of the helix, showing them on the model, explaining how it all works.

"Ten more minutes until the bell rings," she says. "Please continue to quietly discuss your project and make plans to meet after school hours."

"Thanks for standing up for me," Hakim says. "I thought you would be on Pat's side when it came to me."

"Huh?"

"I thought you'd see me as a terrorist too."

"Why would I?"

"I don't know. Because you're Jewish and Israeli, and I'm Muslim?" He's not looking at me. He wraps his fingers in the edges of his T-shirt. "By the way, I'm American. I was born here."

"I don't judge people by where they were born, or where their parents were born, or by their religion," I say.

"I'm sorry. I've never met anyone from Israel before. And I've heard . . ." He stops.

"You've heard what?"

"Never mind—you're right. I was judging. I was generalizing, just like Pat. Sorry. I really am."

I wonder what he's heard about Israelis, but I don't think he'll tell me. I know that some people in the world don't like us. Abba says some people form an opinion about all Israelis based on actions of the Israeli government.

"Anyway, nice to have you as a science partner," Hakim says, smiling.

I smile back, feeling certain that we can get along even if Israel and Iraq do not.

"We only have four and a half minutes left to discuss how, when, and where we're doing this," Chris says.

Jenny returns, all smiles, explaining to Mrs. Adams that she excused herself to the bathroom while she was gone.

"Okay, okay," Hakim says. "My house, Monday after school, and let's make the helix out of candy."

"I can't do Monday," Jenny says, "especially not with candy. And neither can Shai."

"You're deciding for me?" I snap at Jenny.

"It's Yom Kippur!" she says. "What kind of Jew are you?" Chris and Hakim both stare at me.

"Oh, that's right. Sorry, I forgot," I say. "It is Yom Kippur, which means we're supposed to . . ." I'm looking for the word in English— "um . . . fast." It sounds weird. Why couldn't they make up a different word in English for not eating? "Slow" would make more sense. Not eating makes you slow.

"I wouldn't last a whole day without eating," Chris says.

"It's just one day," Hakim says. "Ramadan is a full month of fasting."

"Yeah, but Yom Kippur is twenty-five hours straight," I say. "In Ramadan you start at sunrise, but after the sun sets you can eat all night, right? I guess you've got it harder overall, though, since it's a whole month."

Hakim smiles, with both sides of his mouth. "Most people know nothing about Ramadan."

"*I* wouldn't know that," Jenny says and looks at me like she's accusing me of something. We are so done being friends, and the feeling is clearly mutual.

"Okay, we have two minutes left to decide the details," Chris says.

"Jeez. Chill," Hakim says. "It's due after Thanksgiving, and it's not even Halloween yet. Let's do it over Thanksgiving break." He turns back to me. "So do you have dates after the fast is over?"

"You're asking her out on a date? Dude!" Chris says too loudly.

Mrs. Adams looks our way. "The bell will ring soon," she declares.

Chris elbows Hakim. "You should only be discussing your project."

Heat crawls up my cheeks.

"Not that type of date," Hakim says in a high-pitched voice. "I mean, do you *eat* dates? You know—the sweet fruit that looks like a cockroach."

"You mean tamar." I'm relieved. "Is that what it's called? Date?" Can English be any more confusing? "Yes, we do eat them when breaking the fast. And I always thought they looked like cockroaches too."

Hakim laughs. I like his laugh. It sounds like an explosion of happiness.

* * *

Ema said we shouldn't go to school on a holiday, especially Yom Kippur. Oof. I'll have to make up everything I miss. Abba says there aren't enough Jews in San Diego to justify closing public schools for the Jewish holidays like they do in New York. He could have sent us to a private Jewish school.

I wake up around nine and pull out my sketch-book. I should work on the drawing for the competition now, before I get too hungry to concentrate. I open the sketchbook and grab my colored pencils. I generally prefer markers, but not in my sketchbook. I made that mistake once—my drawing bled to the other side of the paper. And when I turned all the accidental dots on the next page into flowers, it bled right back to the previous page.

I draw the earth and color it in using green and blue. I draw a peace sign over it. I like the round shapes merging, but it's probably been done a million times. I draw the earth again. And again, in slightly different variations, coloring in all the details just to pass the time. I draw kids of all colors circling the earth. So unoriginal. Peace is hard to draw—especially with an empty stomach hinting lunchtime. I have to nail this. I need those plane tickets.

I miss Yom Kippur in Israel, when the world seems to stop for a day. All shops and restaurants are closed. No cars in the streets. Even people who don't fast don't drive on Yom Kippur. The neighbors gather together. The streets are filled with kids on their bikes. For children it's the bike holiday. I put away the sketchbook and drag myself out of bed. Creativity and hunger don't go together.

As I come down the stairs, I hear Ema yelling at Abba that he forgot to cancel the gardener who's working in the backyard, making noise on Yom Kippur. She walks past me, shoving cotton balls in her ears declaring she's going to read in bed, taking her usual Yom Kippur headache with her. Saba complains there's no synagogue in walking distance, and he won't drive on Yom Kippur.

Safta always says Yom Kippur is Satan's day off, a day we rise to the level of angels and go beyond physical needs like eating and drinking. I want to eat so badly, which makes me feel very un-angel-ish. It's also supposed to be a day of forgiveness, but it just feels like everyone is mad at each other.

Safta sets up the Monopoly board—the new English version that Ema got—but Gili argues she prefers our old Hebrew one. Looks like Abba, Saba, and Safta are too hungry to argue.

"The fact that it doesn't feel like it's Yom Kippur means we have to do more to keep the tradition," Safta says.

Gili runs to the kitchen and comes back crunching an apple. She still has a few years until her bat mitzvah, so she's not fasting anyway.

The *crunch* sound of Gili's apple is stuck in my mind, making my mouth water. But Safta is right: fasting is our only connection to the holiday now. I go back to my room and fly-flop on the bed. I do that a lot now that the cast is off.

I open the sketchbook again.

I look at the earth and the peace sign I drew before—round things symbolize the circle of life, like the round challah. My stomach is screeching. I draw more round foods: an apple, a bagel, a donut. Bad idea. I'm so hungry. I draw dates and add little legs turning them into cockroaches, to scare away my appetite. It doesn't help. I guess I should just go downstairs and play Monopoly.

Satan's day off is a very long day.

CHAPTER 20

SAINTS, RED VELVET DIARY, AND PAPIER-MÂCHÉ

The whole neighborhood is wrapped in spookiness. Skeletons and spider webs and pretend plastic graves. Creepy, bizarre decorations. Kay-Lee and Zoe's house has them too.

I've seen Halloween on TV, but I never imagined people really decorated like that. I love it. Saba hates it. I hate that he and Safta are leaving before the holiday, but I can't wait for trick-or-treating.

"It's a Christian holiday," Saba says.

"I think it's completely secular," Ema says.

"It's just a fun, running-around-in-costumes-and-getting-to-know-your-neighbors festivity," Safta says. "Let the kids experience all aspects of living in a different place. Let them have a taste of this culture."

"A culture that tells kids 'stranger danger' all year, and then contradicts itself one day a year by letting them accept candy from strangers?" Saba says. "Do you even know the meaning of the term *Halloween*? All Hallow's Eve is the night before All Saint's Day. Saints.

What saints? It's Christian, I tell you. Next thing you'll have my grandkids celebrating Christmas. I would have sent them to a Jewish school."

"It's not up to you," Ema says.

Safta comes up to him real close. "Come on, Rami. One night of fun won't hurt your Jewish grandkids." Here comes her magic stunt. She stands on her tippy-toes and kisses him on his bald head. When she does that, he forgets what he was mad about, and he agrees to have it her way.

I start singing "Dancing Queen." Maybe it'll help melt his anti-Halloween heart.

Saba grabs Safta's hand, and they start dancing. "Twice as sweet," says Saba.

"That's sweeter than all the trick-or-treat candy," Gili says.

"Experience the culture, you say?" Saba ruffles Gili's hair. "Oh, well. As long as I'm not paying the dental bill." Safta kisses him again.

The house is going to be so quiet without them.

Before leaving to take Safta and Saba to the airport, Ema sets the table with all kinds of chocolate and maple syrups for Saturday's leftover-challah French toast, but I can't eat anything.

Making Halloween costumes with Kay-Lee and Zoe will be a good distraction.

Zoe wants to be a turtle for Halloween. Kay-Lee wanted to sew something for her, but Zoe has been collecting pictures of turtles and doesn't want to hear of any other costume ideas. Ema has volunteered to help make the shell. She loves making costumes, and this should make up for her disappointment that Gili is insisting on wearing her store-bought Dora the Explorer outfit.

Kay-Lee brings a bunch of old newspapers like Ema asked. We use some to cover the table in our backyard. The rest we cut into tiny pieces to make the turtle's shell from papier-mâché.

"It works best with wallpaper paste," Ema says. "I think I have some in one of my unpacked boxes in the garage. Shai, would you check?"

There are a few unpacked boxes in the garage. Two are labeled "Ema."

I open one. Right on the top, there's a red velvet notebook engraved with intricate golden flowers. I stroke it with my fingers. I lift it, looking for the wallpaper paste, which is probably not in this box. I should move on to the next box, but the velvety notebook intrigues me. I randomly open it to the middle. I stare at the beautiful handwriting. Hebrew letters. I shut it. Is it a diary? If I wrote a diary, I would be so mad if anyone even touched it. I stroke the red velvet cover. I bring it up to my nose. It smells of dust, but not exactly. Maybe dust from somewhere far away. It smells like stories that want to be told. It's probably just my imagination. I lay it back in the box.

I find the wallpaper paste in the bottom of a second box, under a mess of other jewelry-making supplies.

In the backyard, Ema is holding up a big laundry basket against Zoe's back. "This will do," she says. I hand her the wallpaper paste, and she blends it with the shredded paper and some white glue. She lets Zoe and Gili mix it all. I almost throw up from the stench, but judging by the smile on Zoe's face, she's happy to have it all over her hands. Ema shows them how to spread the yuck-mix on the laundry basket.

Kay-Lee points at the basket. "Isn't this going to be too heavy?"

"When the layers of paper dry, we'll peel it off the basket. She won't be carrying the basket on her back," I tell her. "It'll be light, and it won't stink so much after it dries." I'm pinching my nose shut.

So is Kay-Lee. "Maybe we should work on your costume at my house," she suggests.

"You both can go," says Ema. "Gili and Zoe are help enough. I need helpers with both hands free."

Kay-Lee and I walk away with our fingers still pinching our noses.

I've made an outline of butterfly wings from thin metal wire. Kay-Lee is going to help me wrap it with blue fabric.

She wants to go as a chef. Her dad will give her a chef's hat and apron. Easy. All white is an extreme costume for someone who wears all colors of the rainbow all year.

Halloween costumes make me think of Purim—my favorite holiday. There are still a few months until Purim. If I win the drawing competition, I'll be in Israel by then. I'll get to have two dress-up holidays in the same school year.

On the way to her house, Kay-Lee says, "Zoe loves Ema. I mean, Zoe loves your mom."

"Kids always love my mom," I say, smiling because Kay-Lee called her Ema.

In Kay-Lee's room, I look through her fabric scraps. I find a sheer, almost see-through blue piece of fabric. I hand it to Kay-Lee.

"I'll have to hand sew it," she says. "With the wire structure, I won't be able to use the sewing machine."

"Oh, sorry." I say. "Maybe I'll just glue it somehow." I didn't mean for her to go through so much trouble.

"It's totally fine. I can do it. I'd love to do it." Kay-Lee grabs the fabric and flattens it out on the carpet, laying my wire wings over it. "Your family does so much for us. Zoe wouldn't leave the house before, and now she goes to your house, and she's happy, and your mom is making her a turtle costume. You're the best neighbors we've ever had."

In Israel, we had old Madeline next door. She used to throw a shoe at Motek every time he barked when she was taking a nap. Then I'd have to go and return the shoe, and if the shoe was all chewed up, she'd scream at me, even though it was her fault. She would blend right in with the Halloween-horror scene. I can imagine her house with spider webs and fake graves.

I look out the window. I see Ema with Gili and Zoe, making the turtle shell in the backyard. Zoe leaning into Ema. Ema hugging her.

My eyes wander back into Kay-Lee's room. She's choosing a thread in the exact shade of blue as the fabric. "You're definitely the best neighbors we've ever had too," I say.

I'll miss Kay-Lee when I'm back in Israel.

CHAPTER 21

YELLOW STAR, SILENT SHOES, AND SAD CONFETTI

"Pssst . . . Shai." I turn around.

The boy behind me hands me a tiny yellow note. My heart and stomach meet in the middle, smacking into each other. Is it from Chris? It's probably for Kay-Lee.

"For you," he says. "It's from Pat."

Oh.

It's cut in a weird shape. Not a regular note, for sure.

I unfold it carefully—it's a Star of David. It says JEW in the middle. My heart and my stomach switch places.

"Put it on, Jew," Pat whispers, and Matt laughs. Or maybe it's the other way around.

I sit frozen in my seat. The teacher is so busy with her equations on the board that she doesn't even notice all this going on. I'm glad she doesn't.

I want to walk over to the trash, throw the note away, and walk out of the class. Out of the school. Out of this neighborhood, this city, this country. I want to walk nonstop all the way to Israel. To Saba and Safta. I miss them so much already. I'd tell Saba he was right all along.

But I stay put, longing for the bell to ring. I shove the yellow Star of David deep in my backpack, trying hard to shove the significance of it out of my mind. I can't imagine the humiliation of Jews in Nazi Germany who were forced to wear this.

Focus on the good. Safta's voice echoes in my head. *What good?* I almost yell out loud.

I wish I was back at my school in Israel, although there were people like Pat there too. Everyone was Jewish, but bullies found other reasons to bully.

Except I was never bullied. I never knew what it felt like. Never even thought about it.

* * *

In science, Mrs. Adams is still on her favorite topic—DNA, the recipe for all living things.

"The same four molecules in a different sequence make a cat different than a tree, different than a human." I wish I were a cat on a tree right now.

"DNA is in every one of your cells." Mrs. Adams taps her shoulders and arms like there are DNA ants crawling on her. "It holds the instruction manual for yourself."

I like that. What does my manual say? Artistic, skinny, blue eyes. It also says Jewish.

Pat's Star of David is burning a hole in the bottom of my backpack. In the bottom of my heart. So is the one on my neck.

"So, as humans," Mrs. Adams continues passionately, "ninety-nine percent of our DNA is the same. It's just that one percent that makes us who we are."

Tell that to Pat. That one percent doesn't make me inferior to him—it just makes him a jerk.

* * *

At lunch, I almost tell Kay-Lee about Pat, but the words stick to the bottom of my tongue like gum glued to the sole of a shoe.

She's dressed in shades of blue and purple today. It's bad. Like grape-jelly-on-eggplant bad. I can't help thinking that I would've been on the bullying side of this purple catastrophe if I were back home, and I hate myself for it.

"Is everything okay?" Kay-Lee asks. I guess getting a Jew tag puts a certain expression on your face.

"Yes," I answer, realizing how unconvincing I sound.

"Trick-or-treating with you two was so much fun," Kay-Lee says.

I try to smile, but the corners of my mouth are so heavy to lift.

"I was thinking of how Zoe was a turtle and you were a butterfly—her carrying her house with her wherever she goes, and you just flying all over the place."

I should've been the turtle.

"Am I being too weird and philosophical? Sorry. I'm just trying to distract you from—I'm not sure what exactly."

"Thank you," I say, and I mean it. "What about Gili as Dora the Explorer? Any wisdom analogies for that one?"

"Maybe she likes learning new languages."

"Nah. She just likes the character, and Zoe just likes turtles, and I just like butterflies. But you are cooking some interesting ideas, Chef—you're a perfect match for ChrisFacts."

Kay-Lee gives me a hug. "See you in band," she says.

* * *

Jenny and the M's are waiting near the band room when the last bell rings. Strange. Are they here for Olivia?

Jenny rushes over to me. Her face is all crunched up and way too close to mine.

"Hi," I say.

"Give Olivia her phone back!" Jenny snaps at me. "We know you stole it."

"What?" I look at Olivia. She's looking at her shoes as if they have the answer to why anyone would accuse me of such a thing.

Jenny clears her people-person throat. "You're the only one who knows her locker combination."

"Because I helped a bunch of girls when we first got our lockers?" I can't believe this. "You really think I could possibly remember everyone's combination?" I stare at Olivia, who's still begging her shoes for an answer.

I throw my bag at her shoes. "Check!" I yell at her. She doesn't move. I grab my bag, unzip it, and start emptying it. I stare at the bottom. Pause. And try not to cry.

Jenny snatches the empty bag and shakes it upside down. The yellow Star of David lands softly on the grass.

Hakim approaches. He's holding a cell phone. "Does this belong to any of you?" he asks. "I found it near the girls' dressing room."

Olivia is still hypnotized by her shoes.

"It's Olivia's," Jenny says, snatching it from him and turning her back to me. "Let's go."

The M's and Olivia all follow her. I hardly hold back my tears as I collect my notebooks and return them to my backpack.

Hakim lifts the Star of David from the grass. I rip it out of his hand.

"Pat?" he asks. I nod.

"I know what that is," Hakim says. "Chris and I watched a documentary about the Holocaust. Pat has gone too far this time. You have to report this, Shai. You should take it straight to the principal's office."

I stare at the star in my hand. "Can't you see? That will only make it worse. He'll be punished, and then he'll hate me even more. He'll never stop." I rip the star into tiny pieces until it's just a handful of harmless yellow confetti. "I'd rather ignore him. Pretend this never happened."

"I think you're wrong," Hakim says, "but it's your choice." He collects the yellow confetti from the grass. "Antisemitic jerk," he mutters on the way to the trash can.

One antisemitic jerk. And one mean girl who thought I was a thief. I won't be able to turn that one into confetti.

CHAPTER 22

FROZEN BRAIN, KITTEN, AND LOYAL DOG

"What's wrong?" Ema asks when she picks me up.

"Nothing," I say. I'd rather delete the day's incidents from my mind.

Ema gives me an I-don't-believe-you stare. "Must have been a really tough nothing," she says. "Will frozen yogurt cheer you up? Gili is going to a friend's house for a playdate straight from school."

I shrug. Ema starts the car.

I want to scream-yell-shout-kick-cry: *I hate it here!* I hate Abba and his avocados and this school. But I keep it all in and swallow it up. I don't want to hurt Ema.

* * *

I dig into my chocolate frozen yogurt through the layer of mini marshmallows on top.

"Are you sure you don't want to talk about it?" Ema asks.

I think of her red velvet diary. I'm sure there's

nothing like that in there. Saba's parents, Ema's grand-parents, came to Israel after surviving the Holocaust. They wanted to raise their kids where nobody would ever give them a yellow star. I swallow a spoonful of frozen yogurt, and it gives me a brain freeze. I wish my brain could actually freeze.

Ema looks as sad as I can imagine she'd look if I did tell her. I open my mouth, but nothing comes out. It's like something is pinching my tongue and my stom-ach, saying, "Keep it inside. Talking about it will only make it worse". Even though this could be the easiest way back to Israel. If my parents hear about this, they'll want to leave. Isn't that what I wanted?

I choke on a marshmallow. Ema whacks me on the back twice. I cough.

"Are you okay?" she asks.

"No," I say when I finally stop coughing. "I mean, yes." I wish I could cough out the whole story like it was a mini marshmallow. But I can't. I swallowed it.

I need a genius idea for the peace drawing competi-tion. I'll win it. And I'll leave, and I'll never come back.

* * *

Ema goes to pick Gili up from her playdate. I go upstairs and take off my Star of David necklace. I stare at it for a moment. I kiss it. And I tuck it at the bottom of my sock drawer. I'll never wear it again.

I open my sketchbook to the page with all the food I drew on Yom Kippur. I flip the page and stare at the blankness of the next one. I hold a blue-colored pencil, waiting for the brilliant idea to travel through the pencil and onto the page, but it isn't coming. I slam the notebook shut. "I hate you!" I yell at it, and I head to the garage.

I open the box with the diary. It's redder and velvety-er than I remembered. It's staring at me, begging me to take it in my hands. I don't stop to think if it's right or wrong. I already know it's wrong. But it's stronger than I am.

I open it randomly in the middle, like I did last time. That feels fairer than starting from the beginning. This way it's not like I'm going to read it from start to finish. I'm just peeking.

The handwriting is so pretty, but it's different from what Ema's handwriting looks like today:

A kitten followed me home. I didn't encourage it. He just walked behind me all the way home from school. I took him in and gave him some milk before Ema came back. I know she won't let me keep it . . .

Of course Safta would let her keep the kitten. I close the diary.

Ema doesn't even like cats. She's a dog person. Or maybe she did like cats as a kid. I can't imagine it. I can't imagine Ema being a child.

I put the diary back in the box. I'm relieved that I didn't come across something more personal, like Ema having a crush on a boy who isn't Abba. If I kept a diary, I wouldn't mind if someone read only a small bit about finding a kitten.

Motek follows me around the house when I walk back in from the garage. I think he can smell the guilt, but my secret is safe with him. Dogs are the best at keeping secrets.

Dogs are the best. They don't care if you're Jewish or if you're wearing purple. And they never accuse you of anything. I sit on the stairs. Motek joins me on the ugly beige carpet and licks away my tears.

CHAPTER 23

SAFTA-HARMONY, CHUSEOK, AND CLICHÉS

Kay-Lee says Thanksgiving is about being thankful for everything you have and eating a huge turkey. Also, she says, it's a festive dinner when all the family gets together. That part sounds like Shabbat dinner, which we have once a week.

But a day for being thankful is a pretty cool idea. I try not think about Pat and Jenny and the M's. Whenever I see them, I pretend they don't exist—they do the same. It's easy to ignore Jenny, but thinking of Olivia makes my stomach shrink.

Jenny didn't even apologize for accusing me of stealing Olivia's phone. I wonder how it's so easy for her to pretend it never happened.

But today I'm focusing on the good: I'm thankful for Kay-Lee and Chris and Hakim. And my family. I decide to like this holiday.

I wonder where the turkey part comes from. No teacher at school has explained Thanksgiving. In Israel, you learn about the holidays at school—the historical or Biblical meaning. Maybe American holidays only get covered in elementary school. I'll have to ask Gili if her class talked about it, or if they just did this art project that Ema is now holding proudly.

"This reminds me," Ema says as she pins the handprint turkey to the corkboard in the kitchen, "Mr. Park invited us to celebrate Thanksgiving with them."

"I thought Lily Levi invited us," Abba says.

Oh, no.

"I told you," Ema says. "She invited us after I already said yes to Mr. Park."

Yes! But . . . that means we're celebrating Thanksgiving? "What will Saba think?" I ask.

"Now this one really isn't a religious holiday," Ema says. "It's American."

"Are we American?" Gili asks. The question hangs in the air. Technically we're not. Or can we be Israeli and Americans at the same time? Maybe we're a hybrid like cherry tomatoes. Gili seems almost more American. I'll always be more Israeli.

"It's not about being American," Ema says. "We're simply a thankful family celebrating our thankfulness with friends."

I'm thankful we're going to Kay-Lee's and not to the Levis. I just hope Abba won't start talking about his job.

Kay-Lee's safta is just a little taller than Gili and has the type of smile that makes you feel warm inside. You can't miss that she's Mr. Park's mom.

"Meet Harmony," Kay-Lee says. "*Halmoni* is 'grandma' in Korean, but Zoe calls her . . ." She looks at Zoe. "I mean, used to call her Harmony. So now we all call her that."

Safta-Harmony nods and shakes our hands. The warmth of her hand matches her smile.

There's a huge turkey in the middle of the dining table, surrounded by a lot of small side dishes of food I don't recognize and bowls of rice.

"The turkey is from the market," Safta-Harmony says. "I'm not good at cooking turkey, but we like to have it. It's the American tradition." Her voice becomes louder when she says the word "American." Sounds like pride.

"Everything else, I make," she says. "What I make for Chuseok, Korean Thanksgiving."

"I brought some Israeli salad—cucumbers and tomatoes, onions and olive oil," Ema explains. "And the bourekas are a pastry with cheese filling." She sets the salad and bourekas on the table.

Safta-Harmony is still smiling and bobbing her head. It's possible they don't understand each other's accents.

"Food unites people from all cultures," Mr. Park says.

Sounds like a cliché. Still . . . maybe the food I drew in my sketchbook does relate to peace somehow? Maybe clichés become clichés because they're overused. But they wouldn't be overused if they didn't work.

"Tell us more about Chuseok," Abba says to Safta-Harmony.

"It means Autumn Eve, and it's a three-day festival. Here in America, we celebrate on Thanksgiving. Easier this way. Korean calendar is lunar, so the date changes."

"Just like the Jewish calendar." Ema sounds excited, as if she just found out Chuseok and Rosh Hashanah are long-lost cousins.

"Try the songpyeon," Safta-Harmony says, pointing at something that looks like the kreplach we put in chicken soup. Which is what I expect when I put it in my mouth, but it tastes completely different. It confuses my senses at first, but then they decide it's good even for my picky taste buds.

Safta-Harmony is eating one bourekas after another, making a long "mmmm" sound between bites. "You must teach me to make these triangles," she says to Ema.

"I'd love to," Ema says. It would be nice if Safta were still here. She would like Safta-Harmony for sure. And she could teach Safta-Harmony how to make the bourekas. Safta's bourekas are better than Ema's.

Zoe smiles the whole time we're there, and Gili talks the whole time. Her English is perfect. Chris says language and accents are easier to learn when you're six or seven. It's because of something called synaptic plasticity, which sounds like plastic and Weather Channel talk to me. But it does make sense that this plastic stuff in the brain is more flexible at Gili's age.

When Ema helps Safta-Harmony clear the table, Zoe brings a picture book and hands it to Gili.

"Not that again," Kay-Lee says. She whispers to me, "My grandmother thinks this book will make her start talking."

Gili reads slowly but with a perfectly American accent. The book is about a shy turtle who starts talking when he has to thank the forest animals for throwing him a surprise party.

"You're a doctor, aren't you, Oren?" Mr. Park asks. Oh no, here it comes. "Know anyone in the child development field?"

"I'm not a medical doctor," Abba says, "I'm a biologist."

"My son is racing from one doctor to another," Safta-Harmony snaps. Her warm smile disappears. "He spends too much money. No expert is helping. I am the expert for my granddaughter. She doesn't need doctors or medication. Just love."

A silence takes over, and I hope the subject of what type of doctor Abba is doesn't come up again.

"Did we bring the Krembo for dessert?" I ask.

"We did," Ema says. "I put them in the kitchen." Gili and Zoe shut the turtle book and run to grab the treats.

Gili gives a long explanation of how you should eat them from the top and leave the biscuit for last. "And open them carefully—be careful not to rip the wrapping."

Ema shows everyone how to make Saba's stars from the Krembos' blue foil. Afterward, Safta-Harmony brings out beautiful patterned paper and teaches us how to make origami paper cranes. Step by step. We all try, except Abba and Mr. Park, who are talking about politics.

Mr. Park asks a lot of questions about the conflicts in the Middle East, and Abba sounds happier talking to him about it than he did with Avi Levi. I don't care what they talk about, as long as it's not the conflict between non-GMO croissants and GMO avocados.

CHAPTER 24

CANDY HELIX, KOSHER MARSHMALLOWS, AND WORLD PEACE

We're meeting at Hakim's house to make the DNA model.

I wasn't sure about the candy idea. I told Chris and Hakim that, in second grade, I made a model of Noah's ark from candy. The teacher loved it but didn't love the ants she found in class the next morning. Hakim pointed out that Mrs. Adams said we could make our model out of anything we wanted as long as it showed the double helix properly, and even Chris said he's sure we'll get graded before the ants come.

I bring all the candy that's left over from Halloween. It's starting to taste like science experiment material anyway.

Hakim opens the door and a familiar smell strikes me. My nostrils must be lying. How can it smell like Safta's house here?

"Nice to meet you! I'm Faiza." Hakim's mom hugs me. "Come in, binti, you must be hungry."

Did she just call me *binti*?

"I heard so much about you, Shai," she says. Even her accent reminds me of Safta's. "I hope you're hungry."

"I told you we're just going to work on a project," Hakim says. "You made way too much food, Mama. You overwhelm people." He looks at me.

I stare at the table. I feel like I'm in Safta's kitchen.

"Don't look so shocked," Hakim says. "She always makes this much food."

"She does." Chris shows up from nowhere. "I probably had the same look on my face the first time I came over."

"My grandma is exactly the same." I barely get the words out.

"See?" Hakim's mom says. "Hope you feel right at home, binti."

I smile. I want to say thank you, but I can't talk and hold my tears back at the same time.

"You can't start the project on an empty stomach," Hakim's mom says.

"Can't argue with Faiza," Chris says. "Might as well eat while we wait for Jenny."

First bite of the kebab, and I almost cry again.

"Have some more," Faiza urges. Exactly like Safta. But Hakim is already clearing the table and setting it up for the science project. He brings toothpicks to connect the candy.

I organize the candy by color.

"You all realize that every living thing has its own DNA? Like, *everything*. Everything we eat too," Chris says. He's such a geek. Handsome geek. But Kay-Lee can have him. All this fact-stating is a little much for me.

"Sure, dude, we know," Hakim says.

"You'd be surprised how many people don't know," Chris says. "I just read this article . . ."

The doorbell rings.

"I'll get it, Mama." Hakim beats his mom to the entrance. "Please don't offer any more food," he adds right before he opens the door.

"Hi, sorry I'm late." Jenny bounces in, all dressed up, smelling sweeter than candy. "I was helping at the Jewish community center. We're setting up a huge menorah for Hanukkah."

"Menorah?" I ask. "For Hanukkah?" I intended to ignore her, but this got me.

"Really, Shai?" she asks, in a tone that sounds like *What kind of Jew are you?*

"Oh, you mean a hanukkiah," I say, redeeming my Jewish-ness. "That's actually different from a menorah. A hanukkiah is specific for Hanukkah and has nine branches. A menorah only has seven . . ."

Jenny tightens her mouth like she's sucking on a hard piece of sour candy.

"So, back to DNA." Chris continues with his lecture. "A survey recently asked Americans if they would want to label food that contains DNA. Eighty percent said they would. Eighty percent." He loves percentages.

"Well, of course. I'm surprised its only eighty percent," Jenny says. "I'd want it labeled for sure."

"Don't you realize that *every* food you eat has DNA?" Chris says. "Just shows how clueless people are, wanting to label because of fear and ignorance. No offense, Jenny."

Her sour face doesn't go well with her sweet perfume.

"You should be friends with my dad." Oops. Did I just say that out loud? Big mistake.

"Your dad's a scientist?" Chris asks, sounding like he's about to ask for Abba's autograph next.

"Yeah," I say. "He messes with DNA for a living."

Jenny checks her phone. "We really should start," she says.

"We should have done this at your house, Shai," Chris says.

I'm so glad we didn't.

"We're just building a basic model of the DNA structure," Hakim says. "With candy. We don't need a scientist for this."

Faiza comes in with a bag of marshmallows in her

hand. "Do you want to use these for your project? Or you can just eat them. They're kosher," she says and puts them on the table.

"Mama . . ." Hakim gives his mom a look that says enough with the food, but she's already leaving the room.

"That's nice of her," I tell Hakim, "but we're pretty secular. We don't mind if candy isn't labeled kosher."

Hakim looks at me funny. "You don't eat pig though, right?" He reads my *what does that have to do with marshmallows?* expression. "We always get kosher marshmallows," he adds. "The other types contain gelatin that sometimes comes from pigs, which we don't eat either."

"I really did not know that," I say. I wonder what type the mini ones at the frozen yogurt place are.

"How did you not know that?" Jenny snaps, like she's the top authority for all things Jewish.

"Maybe in Israel they only have this kosher type," Chris says in my defense.

"My mom never buys marshmallows anyway," I say.

"We get only the kosher ones, which are also non-GMO, of course," Jenny says.

Not that again. I look at Chris—he's rolling his eyes.

"Labeling genetically engineered food is another example of people's ignorance. And their fear of change," Chris says. "Did you know that when trains were invented people were afraid the speed would kill them? When fire was discovered, people thought it was witchcraft. Where would we be without fire today?"

"I don't see the connection." Jenny's face turns red. "This is food we're talking about. I don't want to eat anything that's been messed with in a lab."

For once, I agree with Jenny, but I don't say anything.

"Labs mean advanced and controlled biology. Some genetically engineered foods are much safer than non-GMO." Chris is really worked up about this.

"Safe? Are you kidding?" Jenny stands up. She pushes her chair back so hard that it tips backward, hitting the floor. Hakim stands it back up. Jenny gives the chair an accusing look and stands behind it, leaning on its back. "Some of this stuff is straight-up poisonous. I researched it for a school project last year—"

"Well, do your research again," Chris says. "And not just for a debate when you're representing the anti-GMO side."

He might be right. I think of Abba and about poisoning people, and it doesn't add up.

Jenny's knuckles grow red as she holds on to the chair. "It's poisonous! It was tested on rats."

"People are not rats." Chris stays calm. "Coffee

kills insects, but it's harmless to us. Chocolate is dangerous for dogs but . . ."

"Oh, come on!" Jenny leans into the back of the chair like she's begging it to help her argument against Chris. I almost feel sorry for her.

"Do your research again, Jenny," Chris says softly. "It's harmless to humans. That's been tested too."

"Let's get started with our project," Hakim says.

Jenny lets go of the chair, but Chris won't let go of the argument. "Be open to change," he says, now looking at all of us. Hakim and I exchange looks. "Every new technology has met resistance at first. When the telephone was invented—and I'm not even talking about cell phones, just the regular phone—people were afraid it would give them electric shocks."

Jenny's phone chimes. She jumps as if it gave her an electric shock. "I have to go," she says. "Too bad we wasted our time on pointless arguments."

She turns her back to us. "Thanks, Mrs. Bilal," she says to Faiza in a voice that finally matches her perfume.

"Goodbye, binti—and please, call me Faiza." Hakim's mom gives Jenny a quick hug.

"It's not a pointless argument," Chris calls after Jenny.

"Oh, give it up, man," Hakim says. "Let's just get this project going already."

Turns out the Halloween candy I brought isn't going to work for this. It's all hard candy.

Faiza bought the right type: gumdrops, jellybeans, mini marshmallows (kosher) . . . things you can put a toothpick through. And licorice for the sides of the helix ladder.

"Let's do red for adenine, blue for thymine, yellow for guanine, and green for cytosine." Chris says it easily, like he's dividing his friends into sports teams.

Even if I spoke half as fast as he just did, I couldn't pronounce these names. He reminds us which pairs go together and which are not to be paired. I want to say we should switch around the pairs, since the red would look better with the yellow and the blue would work better with the green, but I don't want to mispronounce anything. Plus, Hakim and Chris have already started skewering candy with toothpicks.

We end up not using the marshmallows, so we just eat them, along with the colors we aren't using and my Halloween candy, which I'm not sure is a good idea. By the time I get home, my stomach feels twisted like a double helix.

I lie in bed, crunched on my side, thinking of everything that's swimming in my stomach. Candy, lots of candy. But also kebab and kibbeh-burghul and yellow rice.

It gives me a different kind of stomachache. I grab my sketchbook from the side of my bed. It's become sort of a sketchbook and diary all in one lately. I scribble thoughts in there between the drawings.

Hakim's mom, Faiza, reminds me of Safta, I write.

Like Kay-Lee's dad said—food connects people. That's it. I draw a bowl and color it like a globe. I add a knife and a fork in it.

It's going to look great once I do it with acrylics. The deadline is December 31. I have plenty of time.

My world-bowl-of-peace will win me my way back home.

CHAPTER 25

PRIVATE HOLIDAY, RARE SANTA, AND MERE EXPOSURE EFFECT

The neighborhood is all dressed up again. This time, it's in red and green, reindeers and snowmen. And it all lights up as soon as the sun goes down.

Hanukkah is considered the holiday of lights, but we sure don't have as many lights as the Americans. The only holiday when we decorate the houses in Israel is Independence Day. The Israeli flag hangs from every house and car.

Hanukkah pretty much went by unnoticed here. My friends in Israel were all posting photos of vacations while I was going to school as if it was just any time of the year. Like on Rosh Hashanah, the holiday was just ours, in the worst way possible. When we were still in Israel, I never thought all that buzz of shopping and prepping and everyone wishing everybody Shana-Tova was such a big part of what holidays are all about. I once heard my aunt say that some things are appreciated only when they're gone. I never understood that. Now I do.

Ema invited Kay-Lee and Zoe over with Mr. Park to light the hanukkiah with us. Safta-Harmony came too. She's now a professional dreidel spinner. We started calling her Safta-Harmony, and she liked it.

There are still a few weeks until Christmas, but it's already in the air. I can't decide what's worse—having your private holiday that no one around you celebrates, or having everyone around you celebrate a holiday that isn't yours.

"Sarah cried at school today," Gili tells us over dinner. Sarah is the only other Jewish kid in her class.

"Why?" Ema asks.

"Because Jake Kelley told her that Santa doesn't bring gifts to Jews."

Ema and Abba look at each other.

"I told her that it's just because we don't decorate our houses in green and red, so Santa knows we don't celebrate Christmas and skips our houses," Gili says.

Pretty smart. I don't know what I would say in that situation.

Abba smiles. "Is that what you think?" he asks Gili.

"Well," she says, twirling one of her pigtails with her fingers, "the tooth fairy only brings you something if you leave a tooth under the pillow, so it makes sense if Santa only goes down the chimneys of the decorated houses."

"That's sweet, Gili." Ema sighs. "I never thought about it. It's hard to be Jewish here."

"Being a minority has its challenges," Abba says.

"How *do* you explain Santa's discrimination to Jewish kids without making him sound like the bad guy and without making Judaism sound like an un-kid-friendly religion?" Ema is really taking this seriously.

"This Santa guy gets credit for something he didn't do," I say.

"So does the tooth fairy," Gili says. She knows. We all laugh.

"Well"—I clear my throat—"I'm going to the mall with Kay-Lee to take a picture with Santa Claus."

Gili looks back and forth between me and Ema, her mouth half open.

"She's joking," Ema says.

"No, I'm not. Safta said to embrace the American experience, so I am."

"Go for it," Abba says.

"I think those photo opportunities at the mall are meant for those who take it seriously," Ema says.

"So, you're saying I can't take a picture with some Santa imposter because I'm Jewish?"

Ema smiles. "I guess that would be discrimination. Okay. Embrace the American experience."

* * *

Kay-Lee's dad drives us to the mall. "How are your parents doing?" he asks.

I squirm in my seat. "Um, okay." My mouth rescues me from my head's answer: *My dad is messing with nature, doing what you stand against.* I still haven't mentioned any of it to Kay-Lee. I want to, but what if she won't want to be my friend anymore? What if we get into a big argument over it? I never want to fight with Kay-Lee. Ever.

"Gili doing well at school?" Mr. Park asks.

"Oh, yes. She loves it, and her English is better than mine." Phew. He's moved on to Gili. He's just making small talk, and we're almost at the mall.

* * *

It's so crowded. Kay-Lee tells me people start shopping for Christmas right after Thanksgiving. There's no guard at the entrance like there is in Israel, checking your bag, checking your car. And people here ask if it's scary living in Israel. This feels scarier to me—no security, in a country where anyone can get a gun.

The decorated mall makes me feel like a cheese stick again. I'm not a part of all this. And the holiday music is super annoying. But I will get two weeks off school like everyone else, so that's good.

I tried to convince Abba we should go to Israel on winter break, even though my friends will be in school, but he says it's too expensive and we should wait till summer and go for a longer time. Instead, Abba and Ema are planning a trip to the Grand Canyon with the Levis. Oof.

"Oh my gosh," Kay-Lee says, pointing toward a house-size Christmas ornament. "Look at that line." We walk closer. Inside the ornament sits a chubby, smiley Santa. White beard and red cheeks. Just like in the movies.

"I'm not so sure we want to stand in this line," Kay-Lee says, counting with her eyes how many people are ahead of us.

"Sure we do. Come on." I pull her arm, and we join the line.

There's a little blond boy squirming on Santa's lap. He's dressed in the cutest reindeer outfit, and he's screaming like Gili did when she got her first haircut. His parents are trying to make him laugh by making faces at him, but I don't think he can even see them through the tears.

"I have a picture from when I was two years old, crying on Santa's lap," Kay-Lee says. "And I have one with Santa from every year after, up to two years ago, and I'm smiling in all of them, so there's still hope for this kid."

"It's a nice tradition," I say.

"Safta-Harmony took me every year. She said that

in Korea, people couldn't celebrate Christmas in public, so here in the US she loves the let's-celebrate-big-time-and-sit-on-Santa's-lap thing."

"My great-grandparents had to hide their Hanukkah celebrations back in Poland. Why should governments even care about what holidays you celebrate? I don't get it."

"Yeah," Kay-Lee says. "My grandma says we don't appreciate democracy enough."

The line is moving slowly. I tell Kay-Lee about my idea for the world-bowl-of-peace. "It was kind of inspired by something your dad said."

"That's so original, Shai. You're going to win this thing."

We're getting closer to Santa. From where we're standing now, I can see that his beard is fake. The music is seriously unbearable.

It's finally our turn. We each sit on one of Santa's knees.

"Ho! Ho! Ho! Merry Christmas, girls."

He has one blue eye and one green eye. This is a rare Santa, I think to myself. And I'm the rare kid on his lap, most likely the only Jewish kid in line.

"I'm Jewish," I whisper. I don't know why. My mouth just beat my brain to it.

"So am I," he whispers back with an oniony breath. We both laugh.

Kay-Lee kicks me. "Shhhhh!"

"Smile to the camera," the woman taking the pictures says. She's wearing an elf's hat with a green pompom and a bell. Kay-Lee and I smile. So does the rare Jewish Santa.

"Next!" the elf camera lady yells.

"Don't tell anyone our little secret." Santa winks his green eye and straightens his beard.

"What secret?" Kay-Lee asks.

"He really comes from the South Pole, not the North, like most people think."

"Come on. Tell me." Kay-Lee jumps on my back.

"South Pole," I say. "You can keep the picture when we get it. I hate seeing myself in pictures."

"You? *You* hate seeing yourself in pictures? You're so beautiful."

"Thank you." Kay-Lee thinks I'm beautiful? "I really do look awful to myself in pictures."

"That's only because of the mere exposure effect," she says.

"What's that?" I don't feel stupid when I'm with Kay-Lee. I feel like she won't judge me for not knowing something that she does.

"It's when you develop a preference to something just because you're familiar with it." Kay-Lee sounds as excited as Chris is about DNA. "You know how sometimes you meet someone and don't think they're very pretty at first? But once you get to know them, you change your mind."

My first-grade teacher was like that. She looked like a scary witch to me on the first day of school, but by the end of the year I thought she was beautiful. "Yeah," I say. "I know what you mean. But what does that have to do with me not liking how I look in pictures?" I hate to spoil her excitement, but I really don't get the connection. "I see myself every day in the mirror. I guess I'm used to myself, but still, I don't like how I look in pictures."

"Exactly. So this is when two interesting phenomena meet."

Now she's really all pumped up. People are looking at her. I laugh.

"What?"

"Nothing. You're so excited." And that word—phenomena. Great word. I have no idea what it means. But I don't ask. Right now, I'm more interested to hear why I hate myself in pictures.

"So," Kay-Lee says, "our faces are not completely symmetrical, you know, not even beautiful faces like yours."

"Ha ha. Okay. True. My left eyebrow is higher up my face than my right one," I admit.

"Actually, it's your right one that's higher. But, see, to you it's your left one because you're used to a mirror image of yourself. The rest of the world sees you like you really are, which is what you look like in pictures. But because of the mere exposure effect, you like the mirror-you better than the real-you, because that's what you're used to seeing. Get it?"

Chris would love this. "How do you know all this?"

"Chris." Kay-Lee giggles. "Where else would I learn stuff like that? Last year, he saw that I was disappointed with my yearbook picture and explained it to me. Then he said I should be happy with myself both in the mirror and in the picture."

He definitely likes her. I'm okay with it.

CHAPTER 26
FRIENDSHIPS, MoMS, AND PAPER CRANES

As usual, it's easy to spot Kay-Lee at the lunch tables—she's in blues and purples again, this time with a touch of green. She looks like a peacock. I get closer—a sad peacock.

Should I ask if she's okay? I hate when people ask if I'm okay when I obviously look like I'm not. I sit next to her and offer her my banana. She doesn't want it.

"Banana is the same in Hebrew." I try to distract her from whatever it is she needs distraction from. "It's just pronounced a little differently. *Ba. Na. Na.*"

She shrugs. My attempts to entertain her are failing miserably.

"I can teach you how to write something in Hebrew."

She hands me a piece of paper and a yellow pencil that matches my banana. "How do you write 'I love you' in Hebrew?" she asks.

"It depends," I say. "Are you a girl saying it to a boy, or a boy saying it to a girl, or a boy to a boy or a girl to a girl?" That sounds trickier than I realized.

"Seriously? It wouldn't be the same thing?"

"No. The verb has to take a female or male form, depending on the speaker."

"That's one complicated language."

"Let's just draw a heart instead of writing 'love.' That would make it easier," I say. "The 'I' is the same, and the 'you' is spelled the same, even though it's pronounced differently."

"So how do you know how to read it?"

"You just know by the context, or you add the dotting, which work as vowels in Hebrew. But you only learn those in first grade, and they're only printed in young children's books. Adults don't use them."

Kay-Lee stares at my hand as I write. "So cool that you write from right to left."

She copies what I wrote—the heart looks perfect, the letters not so much.

"Looks good," I say.

"I'm sure it doesn't. You're just saying that to make me feel better." She looks down at her bracelets, shifting them from one arm to the other. I already know it's a sign that something is bothering her.

She looks at me. "My dad might need to close the bakery. It isn't doing well."

I'm not sure what to say. "Maybe I can draw a mural at the bakery. Maybe something colorful would draw in more customers."

"And ruin my mom's black-and-white theme? Ummmm . . ." She finally leaves her bracelets alone. "Sounds good to me, but I'll have to check with my dad. And you have to finish your drawing for the competition first."

"I'm almost done. It already looks so much better than the original sketch in my sketchbook. And I have winter break to work on it. Don't worry. Let's plan the mural. I'll come by tonight so we can brainstorm it."

* * *

Safta-Harmony greets me at the door when I get to Kay-Lee's house. "Come in, Shai. Good to see you. Kay-Lee is just back from the bakery. Helping her dad. Such a good girl."

I go upstairs and find Kay-Lee spread on her bed. Her outfit blends in with the bedspread.

"You know," she says, "I was born in this house." Her eyes are fixed on her feet as they stroke the carpet. "My mom was all about everything natural. Natural birth, natural look, natural food. She's the reason everything in the bakery is made with all-natural ingredients."

"Non-GMO," I blurt. I stare at the carpet as she plows it back and forth with her feet. I swallow hard, trying to keep more words from escaping my mouth. No luck. "She would have hated my dad."

Kay-Lee's plowing feet pause. She lifts her gaze. "What? Why?"

"Genetically modifying organisms is what he does. It's his job. That's what brought us here. I'm sorry." I don't know what to say next. I don't know how to justify Abba—or how to not justify him.

"What are you sorry for?" Kay-Lee says. "I bet GMO can be used for good and for bad. Your dad is a good man, and I'm sure he's an honest scientist. Plus, I'm sure a lot of my dad's customers ask for organic and non-GMO without knowing exactly what it means. He just gives them what they want, doing what's good for his business. That doesn't mean we think everything about GMO is evil."

Now I'm staring at the carpet. She sees Abba as a good scientist, and I was busy thinking the worst of him.

And she's not at all upset with me. All this time I was afraid to tell her. It was just me stuck on being mad at Abba. Like Chris said to Jenny, I only searched for the information I wanted to find.

"Anyway . . ." Kay-Lee's eyes wander back to her feet. "Our dads are both good people. It's my mom who started with the natural-this-natural-that stuff, and then she naturally got up and left us. Like it was natural for a parent to leave her own kids."

"I'm sorry." I'm not sure what else to say. Safta's *Focus on the good* rings in my head.

"You're lucky to be living in the house you were born in," I say. I wish I'd never left the only house I've known as my home. She takes it for granted, like I took the vibe of the holidays for granted when I was still living in Israel.

We just sit together on her bed, not saying anything.

"She went back to France." Kay-Lee breaks the silence. "That's where she's from. The French bakery was her idea—her dream. Now my dad has to manage it all on his own since she took off to chase her new dream: becoming a singer in Paris."

I follow her gaze to the paper-crane letters on the shelf.

"I never read any of these," Kay-Lee says.

How can she not read letters from her mom?

"She's been calling lately, but I never want to speak to her, and Zoe doesn't talk to anyone anymore, which is all our mom's fault. She told my dad she wants Zoe and me to come to France for Christmas. Like nothing happened. Like he can afford two round-trip tickets to France when he's trying to save the bakery."

"Maybe you should . . ." I pause, not sure if I should say what I'm thinking. "Maybe you should read the letters?"

"You don't get it!" she snaps. "I mean, how *could* you get it? With your perfect mom and your perfect family."

I feel myself shrinking to the size of a stitch on her quilt.

"You think I'm lucky to be living in the house I was born in?" She's practically yelling now. "It's just a house. You live with the family you were born with. You don't understand anything. Just go."

"I'm sorry," is all I manage to say.

"Just go."

I leave. And it hurts more than the yellow star, more than the theft accusations, more than all the bad things that happened up until now put together.

CHAPTER 27

BLACK DRESS, SAUSAGE, AND BAKE AN EGG

I never thought I'd be onstage in the front row, holding a trumpet, wearing a dress. Especially the wearing-a-dress part. It's plain and black, but still a dress. My friends in Israel wouldn't believe it.

I stare at Kay-Lee at the other side of the stage where the flute section is. I'm not used to seeing her in black. She's just as pretty as in color. I want to go and apologize, but I'm too "sausage" to do it. In English, it's too "chicken," but my brain works in Hebrew.

Hakim comes backstage with Chris. "Break a leg," he says.

I thought we were friends now. Why would he say something like that?

"The curtain will go up in ten minutes," Mr. Belton says. "You are all going to be fabulously fantastical. Your parents are sitting in the audience expecting a middle-school-level concert, but you all sound like pros. You got this."

I touch the cool metal of the trumpet in my hand

and can't help feeling lucky there was no room in art.

Maybe I just didn't hear what Hakim said, but what else can sound like *break a leg*? Break an egg? Or maybe bake an egg? That doesn't make sense either because who bakes an egg? I'm probably thinking "bake" because I miss Kay-Lee. I'm almost sure he said "Break a leg." Weird.

The curtain rises, exposing a full auditorium. I can't spot my parents, but I feel an energy I can't explain. Like I'm in one of those snow crystal balls that you shake so that the glitter floats all around. I feel the glitter—I am the glitter—wrapped in music. We are all inside a magical crystal ball.

As the audience applauds, I think of Safta. Goodness is in full focus. I wish she and Saba were here for the concert.

Bake an egg, I tell myself.

I spot Olivia in the first row, standing up and clapping. Why is she here? Jenny isn't in band anymore. Our eyes meet for a split second, and I quickly look away. But a second later, I look back at her. She looks nervous, and I decide that if she apologizes about the phone incident, I will forgive her. Safta says you should forgive even those who don't deserve forgiveness because you deserve to move on.

I'm hoping Safta-Harmony has a similar saying she says to Kay-Lee.

Offstage, Ema, Abba, and Gili rush to congratulate me. I spot Hakim, but Olivia is nowhere in sight. Maybe she's a sausage too. I can't blame her. Apologizing is hard.

Hakim gives me a quick hug.

"I thought you told me to break my leg before the concert," I tell him.

He explodes into laughter.

"What?" I slap his arm. "Was it bake an egg?"

He's laughing even harder now, "'Break a leg' means good luck," he says.

That doesn't even make sense. English is so weird.

"Where did Kay-Lee go?" Ema asks on the way back home. "I wanted to congratulate her too. She looked professional up there with her flute, and so beautiful in black."

I don't say anything. I want to tell Ema about the fight, but I don't feel like hearing what she or Abba think of it. I don't want it to become a big deal.

"We should go buy Kay-Lee and Zoe something for Christmas," Ema says.

She's right. And it will force me to go and apologize. I never even got a chance to show her my finished drawing for the world peace competition. I showed it to Ella on Facetime, but she didn't really get it. Kay-Lee got it just from the description before it was even done.

"Maybe we could get Kay-Lee a journal," I say. "Something really nice and fancy to write in. A diary. We can also get one for Zoe. With her not speaking, it can be good for her too."

"That's a wonderful idea, Shai," Ema says. "I wish I had one when I was growing up."

I don't understand. Ema never lies. Could she have forgotten about her red velvet diary? Did she get hit on the head and lose her memory? Would she be mad if I told her I read her diary? I'd be mad if she read mine.

"Maybe we'll also get Krembo for Zoe and Kay-Lee. And for us too," Gili says.

"You're not schlepping me to all your shopping errands," Abba says.

"I wouldn't dare," Ema says, "especially not this time of year with all the Christmas-mania. And Shai probably wants to change out of the dress anyway."

* * *

At the international market, we get a few boxes of Krembo. We also get hummus and tahini and a few other things that taste like home. Next, we go to Target. My favorite store. Gili's too. There aren't any stores in Israel that sell so many different things—bubblegum and furniture, school supplies and hair accessories, toys and vitamins.

First, we choose a diary for Kay-Lee. I want to find a red velvet one to make Ema remember hers, but there's nothing like it. I choose one with a collage of different patterns that reminds me of Kay-Lee's bedcover. Gili chooses a Dora the Explorer one for Zoe. I'm not sure Zoe's going to like it, but Gili insists.

Gili and I run to the greeting card section and start reading cards. I could stay in this section forever, except for the Christmas music. Ema says it's not good to leave the hummus in the car for too long and we're talented enough to make our own cards.

"We can wrap the Krembo in green and red so it's more Christmas-y," I say. Ema and Gili like the idea. We get some wrapping paper and head home.

I bring all my markers and papers to the kitchen table. Gili draws Santa Claus with a blue Star of David on the white rim of his hat. The rare Santa at the mall would have loved it.

Gili might be more talented than I am. I'm not jealous. I'm kind of proud she's my sister.

I draw a Santa too, but with a chef's hat and two girls beside him.

"Wow!" Gili says. "That's so good. I want to draw like you when I grow up."

"You'll draw better than that when you're my age," I say. Gili runs to tell Ema what I said. Nice to see that her tattling isn't exclusively for bad stuff.

My card for Kay-Lee is a Christmas card and an apology card all in one. I hope she forgives me.

When Safta-Harmony opens the door, I get a ping in my brain saying *Why didn't we get her a card too?* She's my favorite safta besides my own. Gili and I tell her we have gifts for the girls.

Zoe runs to the door and hugs both of us.

Safta-Harmony says Kay-Lee is helping her dad at the bakery. She's been spending a lot of time there. If she forgives me, I'll go help too.

But first I'll have to get over my sausage-ness and make things right again with my best friend.

CHAPTER 28

TEARS, TEARS, AND TEARS

It takes me a few seconds to realize that I'm awake and that the phone ringing is not a part of my dream. This can't be a good thing in the middle of the night.

I look at the clock. It's 4:54 a.m. The ringing stops. And starts again.

I hear Abba answering. I can't hear what he's saying, but he's speaking Hebrew.

I jump out of bed and slowly walk down the hall to my parents' room.

I hear Ema saying, "What? What? Who? Oren, what happened?"

I do the math. It's almost 3 p.m. in Israel.

"It's your parents," he tells Ema. My legs root to the floor. I can't move.

Something's happened to Saba and Safta. Nausea climbs up my throat. I don't want to hear, but I can't make myself not listen.

"They were at a restaurant in Tel Aviv," Abba says, "and there was an explosion."

Ema lets out a cry that sends me flying from the

doorway into their bed.

Abba hands Ema the phone. I hear a hysterical version of Aunt Sigal's voice.

Abba hugs me and gives me a kiss on the top of my head. "Saba will be okay," he says. His voice cracks.

What about Safta? I can't bring myself to ask out loud.

He lets go of me and gets up. I put my head in Ema's lap.

Ema's crying into the phone. "But she'll be okay, right? She'll be okay?" I've never seen her cry like this. It scares me.

Ema hangs up the phone. She's still crying and rubbing my back.

"She can't die," I say. Which makes her cry even harder. She keeps rubbing my back in strong circular motions, almost as if a genie is going to come out of me and she can make a wish. I wish I had the power to make her wish come true. I wished too hard to go back. It's all my fault.

Abba returns, carrying his laptop. "The soonest flight I can find for you leaves from Los Angeles at 1:30. I'll drive you after we drop the girls off at school." His eyes are locked on the computer screen. He's switched to practical mode. Ema is still in sobbing mode.

"I want to go see Safta," I say.

Ema stops rubbing my back. I sit up.

"Shai." Abba gets up and sits next to me. "I'm sorry, honey."

He hugs me. I try to break free from his hug, but he holds tight. Eventually he loosens his grip just a little and looks into my eyes. "Go back to bed. Try to get some sleep. School's in just a few hours."

"I'm not going to school! And do you really think I can fall asleep now?" I'm screaming. At my dad. In the middle of the night.

Abba reads from his laptop: "Seventeen people killed and forty-eight injured in an attack at Pizza Nitza in Tel Aviv this afternoon. Four children and one three-month-old baby are among the dead."

"Stop!" I yell. I cover my head with the blanket. But I can still hear him reading like it's just another article from the news that doesn't involve anyone we know.

Except this time it does.

"That's enough," Ema says. The room becomes quiet.

Through the shutters, more light starts coming in. How can the sun be rising when all this is happening?

Only the sound of Ema's sobs cut the silence.

* * *

Safta is in the hospital. In a coma. I don't exactly know what that means, and I'm scared to know, but Gili asks, and I decide I should listen when Abba answers.

He says Safta is in a state of unconsciousness. She can't move or feel or speak or hear.

"So she's like Sleeping Beauty," Gili says.

"She doesn't respond to light or sound. Not even to pain." Feels like he's talking to himself now.

"It's good to not feel pain," Gili says.

If Safta's *Focus on the good* is genetic, it's definitely on Gili's DNA helix.

I can't face school, and Abba doesn't make me go. Winter break starts in two days anyway.

Lily Levi brings us some home-cooked meals. I like her, even though her husband is a jerk and her daughter is boring and obnoxious. They're going to the Grand Canyon without us. I've convinced Abba that we should go to Israel.

Ema loves the idea. She says having us there and hearing our voices might help Safta come out of the coma.

A voice inside my head yells, *You got it all wrong! Not like this.* I wanted to go home, and I didn't want to go on the trip with the Levis, but Safta was not supposed to get hurt. Maybe I wished too hard.

"Who will watch Motek while we're gone?" Gili asks.

"We can ask Kay-Lee and Zoe," I say.

"Good thinking, Shai," Abba says. "Let's go talk to Mr. Park and the girls."

"I'll go," I say. I don't know if Kay-Lee saw my Christmas-apology card yet. But this is my chance to apologize face-to-face. Abba gives me the spare keys to the house. I can give them to Mr. Park if he and the girls say yes to taking care of Motek.

Kay-Lee opens her front door a second after I knock. Like she's been waiting. She gives me a hug that's more strangling than Saba's hugs. I can't breathe. Finally, she lets go, and I'm breathing better than I have been ever since our fight.

"I meant to come over. I got your card . . ." she says.

"I'm sorry," I say.

"No. I am." She grabs my hand and leads me up the stairs.

"My grandmother was hurt in a terror attack," I say. "She's in a coma."

"Safta?" She stops and comes down one step to the one I'm on. She hugs me again. This time it's a soft hug. A butterfly-wings sort of hug. I shut my eyes. Tears trickle down my face and reach my mouth so fast that it takes me a moment to recognize where the saltiness is coming from.

"I'm sorry," Kay-Lee whispers. "I'm sorry about everything." After a minute we keep going up the stairs to her room.

First thing I notice is that there's a row of blue-foil stars instead of the paper-crane letters on the shelf. I smile. Saba's famous stars that Ema showed Kay-Lee and Zoe how to make. They must've eaten all the Krembos already.

But where are the cranes?

Kay-Lee looks back and forth from me to the shelf. She picks up a pile of geometrically grooved papers. The letters. All flattened.

"She had a mental health crisis," Kay-Lee tells me. She says the words carefully, as if they're new to her. "My mom. She was diagnosed with a mental illness. I didn't know. All these years I didn't read her letters. I didn't know what she was going through. All this time I was too busy being mad. If it wasn't for you, I still would be. Thank you," she says, hugging me again. "Safta will be okay. I'm sure of it."

I wipe away my tears and nod.

Focus on the good.

CHAPTER 29
ARABIC, BITTER TEA, AND HUGS

It's agreed that Kay-Lee and Zoe, with the help of Mr. Park, will feed and walk Motek while we're gone. Safta-Harmony promised to help too.

All that's left is to pack. As I toss clothes into my suitcase, I see my drawing for the competition. I don't have time to scan and send it—I'll miss the deadline. What's the point now anyway? I'm going to Israel tonight. I'll stay next to Safta's hospital bed and never come back.

I miss Ema. That's my excuse to sneak out to the garage and pull out the velvet diary. I open it randomly in the middle again, still feeling it's the right way to do this wrong thing.

I can't read it. I don't understand. It's not Hebrew— these beautiful ornamented letters, they're Arabic. The writing also goes from right to left, but it's nothing like Hebrew. I close the diary and sink my face in the dusty velvet. Half the blood in my body goes up to my head, the other half down to my feet. Everything in between feels empty.

It's not Ema's. It's Safta's.

But why does Ema have it?

I sit on the floor and open the diary to the very first page. Arabic. Safta probably started writing it when she was still in Iraq. I turn the pages like they're made of thin glass. About halfway through, I reach the point I can read:

This is my home now, and Hebrew is my language. From now on I will write only in Hebrew, even if I write with many spelling mistakes.

There are lots of spelling mistakes in those two sentences. I keep reading.

In Baghdad, the kids called us Jews, but here in Israel where we're surrounded only by Jews, the kids call us Arabs. I want to be one of them, the Israeli kids. I will never again speak or write in Arabic. From now on, I'm Israeli.

I feel so close to Safta now—and yet so far. I hug the diary to my chest and run out of the house.

At first, I don't know where I'm running, but eventually my legs send an update to my brain. I'm on my way to Hakim's house. I need to see his mom. She can translate the diary for me.

I catch my breath before I knock on the door.

Faiza opens the door. "Shai, hello. Hakim isn't home, but come in." She scans me from head to toe. "Everything okay? You look a little pale, binti."

Binti. My heart stops pumping blood. My eyes start pumping tears. Faiza hugs me. My tears stain her shirt. I step away from her hug, and she lifts my chin.

"My grandmother's in the hospital," I say.

"Come in. I'll make some tea."

I sit in the living room and stare at the diary in my lap.

Faiza comes back with a tray and sits next to me. "Drink, binti." She hands me a cup, decorated with tiny gold flowers around the rim.

I lift the cup in slow motion, afraid to spill tea on the diary. I take a little sip. It's bitter, but I don't want to insult her, so I drink a little more before I lower the cup back onto the table. I stroke the red velvet. "It's my grandmother's diary, from when she was a kid in Iraq," I say.

Faiza cups her knees with the palms of her hands and squeezes them—kneading them as if they're dough, as if she's trying to sculpt them into some other shape.

I take a deep breath. "I hoped you could translate some of it for me." I want to suck the words right back into my mouth the moment they leave it.

Faiza lets go of her knees and claps her hands together softly. She lets out a silent sigh.

"Sorry." I hug the diary. "This is wrong. I shouldn't ask you to read someone else's diary. I shouldn't be looking at it myself. I'm a bad person for taking it."

"Good people do wrong sometimes. But if they feel bad about it, it's a sign that they are still good. You're a good girl, Shai. You listen to the ticking of your conscience and the whispers of your heart."

I let the tip of my tongue stick out just enough to catch a tear that has reached my lip.

"Binti, you love your grandma and her life is in danger. I do not judge you. You want to feel closer to her now." She kneads her knees again. "Where did you find the diary?"

"In a box with some other stuff that belongs to my mom."

"Well, my guess is that if your mom had it, your grandmother meant for the diary to be passed on. I could be wrong, but that would be a rarity." She laughs. Just a quiet, gentle laugh, like she's trying to release tension from this awkward situation. It's working. "So, what do you say? Should I translate just a bit? I'll be your partner in crime if you promise to tell your grandmother we took a peek once she wakes up."

If. If she wakes up. I look into her deep brown eyes and raise my gaze to her graying hairline. Not if, when. *When* Safta wakes up. I force myself to believe it.

Maybe reading to Safta from the diary could help get her out of the coma. I could bring it to Israel with me. "Let's read," I say.

I find the last page that's still in Arabic, just before the Hebrew starts, and I hand it to Faiza. She takes the diary from my hands like it's a jeweled crown and slowly reads aloud in Arabic. Then she translates:

What makes a home a home? Baghdad was my only home—and my parents' home before I was born. Is home the place you were born? The place where your parents raise you? Any place where your parents take you?

Faiza stops reading and looks up at me, like she's waiting for me to tell her if she should keep reading. When her eyes lock on mine, she shuts the diary. "Your grandmother was asking the same questions you're asking. Am I right, binti?" She strokes the red velvet.

I nod, sticking out my tongue to catch another tear.

"I asked the same questions when I came to America," Faiza says, handing me the diary. "There is no single, simple answer. But at the same time, it is not as complicated as it first seems. You will find your answers." She hands me a tissue, and I wipe my tears. "And your grandma is going to be okay," she says. "I feel it in my bones."

I force a smile, but as the corners of my mouth lift, it stops feeling forced. Faiza deserves a smile.

"Hakim should be back in an hour. Do you want to wait for him?"

"No, thanks. I need to get going. We're leaving for the airport soon. Just tell him I said hi."

We both get up, and Faiza gives me a hug. I sink into her, aware that I might be stuck in this hug for too long. But when I break away, she hugs me again.

As I walk home, I think about hugs—how much power they have. Maybe there'd be no terror attacks if there was more hugging in the world. It's a very childish and naive thought, but I'd like to hang on to it anyway.

CHAPTER 30

THE AIR OF HOME, THE SMELL OF HOSPITAL, AND A SPRINKLE OF HOPE

Everyone claps when the wheels of the plane touch the ground. That's the sound of Israelis landing in Israel.

We're home. I don't know what I'm feeling right now. I want to just be happy, like I'd always imagined I'd be when I came back. But I'm dreading the moment Abba turns on his cell phone after the fifteen-hour flight. What if Safta is dead? I force that thought out of my head.

Safta's diary is burning a velvety red fire in the bottom of my carry-on bag. I thought maybe reading to Safta from the diary would help wake her up, but how do I explain to Ema that I brought it? That I found it. That I figured out it was Safta's.

I look at Gili. She's asleep.

"Wake up, Gili," I say. "We landed. We're home. You have to put your shoes on."

Her eyes are red when she opens them. Sleeping on a flight is the worst kind of sleep.

Ema is waiting for us at the airport. I don't recognize her at first. Her eyes are red too. Not like Gili's, from sleeping on a flight. More like from not sleeping at all. But when Gili jumps on her, wrapping her with tiny arms and legs, Ema's red eyes shine.

"I missed you all so much." She puts Gili down and hugs Abba and me.

"How's your mom?" Abba asks.

"Not good. No change. Not good."

Sometimes people say the same thing twice when they need to keep talking, when there's nothing else to say. Not good. Twice. That's twice as bad as just one "not good."

"I hope all the luggage fits in the car," Ema says. Small problems are easier to deal with.

When we step out of the airport, I feel home on my skin. The air of Tel Aviv. Maybe it's the humidity? The sunlight hurts my eyes. It's nighttime in California. My stomach hates jet lag. It feels like it's been combed from the inside.

"Let's drop the luggage off at home first," Ema says, meaning at Saba and Safta's house. "And then we'll go to the hospital."

It's weird that she's driving Safta's car.

"Will Safta even recognize us?" Gili asks.

Ema sighs and keeps her eyes on the road as Abba runs his hand through her hair.

Gili's question hangs in the air. I open the window, hoping it will fly out. But I can feel it still hanging. Fastening a seatbelt. Echoing in my ears.

"Why did that man blow up in the restaurant?" Gili asks. Again. I want to hug her, but our seatbelts stand in the way. I feel a tear trickle down my cheek.

"Because he is a very bad man," Abba says, dropping his hand from Ema's hair. He stretches his seatbelt, turning his head around to look at Gili. He's already explained to her that some people use violence to try to scare other people.

"Maybe flowers instead of bombs," she says. Gili is so naive. She would believe my hug theory too. I wish six-year-olds were in charge of everything. They would rule the world with flowers and balloons and sweet cotton candy, and there would be nothing to fight but tooth decay.

Abba reaches his hand to the back seat and holds Gili's hand.

"I'm so glad you're all here," Ema says. I can't see her face from where I'm sitting, but her voice sounds like she's crying. She looks sideways at Abba. "Thank you."

I can see her shiny, wet cheek now.

Gili curls into a ball, rests her head on my shoulder, and falls asleep.

* * *

I flop onto the living room sofa when we arrive at my grandparents' apartment. I shift my butt to the familiar sunken spot that has probably been created from years of use. I hug the fluffy pillow with the red roses. I bring it to my nose and inhale the mango-ish smell of Safta.

Ema opens the shutters, letting the sun in. Tiny dots bounce frantically in the air and blur my vision.

"Come on, everyone," Abba says. "We're all tired. Let's go to the hospital just for a short while. I'm sure Saba will be very happy to see you girls."

"I'll stay with Safta tonight," Ema says. "Saba hasn't let me or Sigal take his place for a week now. Hopefully tonight he'll agree to get a good night's sleep in his bed. Having his granddaughters here should do the trick."

My grandparents really love each other. I only thought of her, but now I worry about him. I can't imagine Saba without Safta.

On the way to the hospital, everyone is silent. I lean against the car's window. Everything's so much smaller than in San Diego. And less groomed. Like the gardener is slacking and the streets need repaving.

Cars cut each other off left and right. Was it always like that? Only the metal ram's head sculpture in front of the Museum of Art looks the same as I remember it. The museum itself looks smaller, and the palm trees next to it look like dwarfs compared to the ones in California.

My twin cousins are playing in the grass at the hospital entrance. When they run to hug us, it feels like the wrong thing, at the wrong place, at the wrong time.

"Gili," Ema says, "maybe you should stay here and play with the twins."

"No," Gili says. "I want to see Sleeping Beauty Safta."

We all go inside. The corridors are too bright, the faces too sad. The smells are a mixture of bad food and medicine and pee. This place is evidence of all the bad that is in the world. I hate hospitals. *Focus on the good*, Safta's voice almost yells at me in my head. Okay. I'll try. Doctors and nurses save lives here, so it's a good place.

I still want to turn around and run out of here, past my cousins playing on the grass and across King Saul Boulevard to the museum, where there's only art around. Inside the museum, you don't have to think about the real world.

I used to take classes there. I know my way around the Tel Aviv Museum of Art with my eyes shut. I know exactly where I'd go now if I could. Straight to Jackson Pollock's *Earth Worms* painting. I always loved staring at that spaghetti tangle. If I stare at it long enough, I bet I can pretend to be part of the picture.

"Shai?" I feel Ema's hand on my back. The elevator is here.

* * *

When I see the tubes coming out of Safta's nose and arm, I think of the Jackson Pollock worms again.

"Maybe it wasn't a good idea to bring Gili in here," Abba whispers to Ema.

Gili goes straight to Safta and holds her hand. The tubes don't seem to bother her.

We all hug Saba. He barely hugs back. I miss his squishing hugs.

I move closer to Safta's bed and start singing "Dancing Queen." Very quietly. Her eyes open for a second and close again. I stop singing.

"Don't stop," Ema says.

I continue singing. When I get back to the chorus, Saba says, "Twice as sweet," and his voice cracks.

My throat closes up. If he cries, I'll die on the spot, right here on the hospital floor.

I run out of the room all the way to the elevators. Ema comes after me.

Feels like the world is spinning—as if gravity is about to forget to do its job.

"Come on," Ema says. "You had a long day. You should try to get some sleep. Tomorrow you can see your friends when they get back from school."

Saba catches up with us. "Shai." He grabs my shoulder. "I hope you realize it's a big deal that Safta opened her eyes when you sang to her."

I didn't.

I look at Ema. Did she realize?

Her eyes are a little wet. Maybe it's glimmers of hope.

CHAPTER 31

DAWN WITH SABA, BAGGED CHOCOLATE MILK, AND A LOAD OF HOPE

I blame jet lag for waking me up when it's still dark outside. Saba's snoring isn't synchronized with the chirping of the crickets.

I sneak into Saba and Safta's room and lie on Safta's side of the bed. I sink my face into her pillow.

"Shai?"

Did I fall asleep? Saba's voice wakes me up. Still dark outside.

"Do you want to come to the hospital with me?" he asks.

I rub my eyes.

"Just the two of us," he says. "The others can join later."

I get dressed quickly for what feels like an adventure with Saba—a mission to save Safta. Like only the two of us together have the power to do it.

We leave the house on tippy toes. Like burglars.

Saba stops for coffee on the way. Shades of red color the sky. Saba gets us croissants—plain for him and chocolate for me. You can't find croissants this good in America, not even in Mr. Park's bakery. Not even in France, Saba says.

Even Avi Levi admitted that he misses the food in Israel, and he hates everything about Israel.

Saba also gets me shoko besakit. I've missed that. In America, you can only buy chocolate milk in a bottle or in a carton. Chocolate milk in a little plastic bag is the best. I bite off the corner of the rectangular bag and lock my mouth on the opening, squirting delicious chocolate milk into my mouth.

The sun is fully out when we get to the hospital. The grass at the entrance seems empty without my cousins running through it.

Safta is still wrapped up in ugly hospital pajamas. Ema is asleep on the chair next to her.

"Neta'le." Saba strokes Ema's hair like she's still his little girl. She opens her eyes. "Go home, dear. Get some sleep. Shai and I are here now," Saba tells her.

Ema hugs both of us and strokes Safta's hair just like Saba did to her a minute ago. "See you later," she says softly and leaves.

Saba kisses Safta's forehead. It's a gentle kiss, like he's afraid to break her.

"Look, Aviva," Saba whispers. "Our beautiful Shai is here." He takes my hand, leading me closer to Safta's bed. "Talk to her," he says. "Say anything that comes to your mind. Just so she hears your voice." He kisses the top of my head. "I'm going to talk to the nurses."

The diary. Oof. I forgot it.

I hum "Dancing Queen" and stroke Safta's hand. Her nail polish is peeling off. My focus-on-the-good grandma isn't focused on anything. It's up to me to focus for her. I tell her all about reading her diary, and I keep stroking her hand. She remains a statue. A statue of my Safta.

"When did you start feeling Israel was home, Safta?" I whisper. "The kids here called you an Arab, but the kids back in Iraq spit on you for being Jewish." I squeeze her hand and tell her about Pat and about the yellow Star of David. I finally let out the mini marshmallow that's been growing in my throat.

I don't know if she's hearing any of this. Her eyes slowly open, but they close again right away. Maybe I imagined it. I turn around. Saba is standing at the entrance, wiping a tear. He comes close to Safta and runs his fingers through her hair.

How long has Saba been standing there? How much did he hear?

He turns from Safta to me. "Always be proud of who you are," he says. That's when he looks at my neck. "Where's your necklace?"

I run my fingers across the spot where it used to dangle.

"It was wrong of me to tell you not to wear it." Saba comes around and puts his hands on my shoulders. "The Nazis marked us to identify us, to humiliate us. But if we choose to mark ourselves, we do it with pride. If anyone has a problem with your Star of David necklace, it is they who should feel ashamed, not you."

I look at my sleeping Safta. Her parents came to Israel because they felt unsafe amongst Muslims in Iraq, but the hate they feared exists here too—that's what put her in this situation.

"Do you think all Muslims are bad?" I ask Saba.

He pulls another chair next to Safta's bed. He bends his knees in slow motion, lowering himself cautiously into the chair. "Of course not," he says. "Being good or bad has nothing to do with race or religion."

"I have a Muslim friend in America, and he's a very good person," I say.

"Binti." A soft whisper comes from the bed. "I had Muslim friends."

We both look at Safta.

"In Iraq."

She talked!

Saba lowers his head toward Safta. He brings his head to her heart. She moves just a little and gives him a kiss on his bald head.

CHAPTER 32

FALAFEL, CLAY HEARTS, AND HOME

There's still some swelling in Safta's brain. Fluid is pushing against the skull, the doctors say. Ema says it's a long way to full recovery, but at least she's out of the coma.

Safta needs to rest, so Abba takes us out to eat at his "best falafel place." Every Israeli has a different falafel place they consider the best. I don't care which one we go to as long as the pita is good, and you can count on that everywhere in Israel. It's not the thin, dry pita like in America. Here, the pita bread is thick and easy to open, like a pocket, and it holds the falafel, the hummus, and the salad without breaking.

Abba complains the whole way about the crowded roads and the rude, honking drivers. I hate that he sounds like Avi Levi.

Someone snatches the parking spot he was about to park in. "Israelis!" he yells, but right away he finds a spot not too far from the falafel shop.

"I could eat this every day." I lick the tahini spilling from the side of my pita.

"I forgot how good the food is here," Abba sighs, finally saying something positive about Israel. But as soon as we're back in the car, he loses his temper again. "Nobody has patience in this country," he yells when someone cuts him off while switching lanes.

Maybe Avi Levi was right. I want to erase this thought out of my head. I look out the window. I love that all the signs are in Hebrew. I used to be oblivious to that.

Maybe it's the mere exposure effect that makes me love Israel so much. Maybe it's just because I'm used to it, because I've spent most of my life here, that I believe it's the best place on earth. I think of Kay-Lee and Hakim, Mr. Belton and band, and the summer that feels like air conditioning. I think of all the things I wanted to hate when I thought I didn't belong. Maybe I belong in two places at the same time.

I wish I could see my three best friends all together, but Ella and Tal aren't talking to Shir. Some fight over a boy.

Ella says I was the glue. I don't have time to glue them all back together again. I'm only here for a week, and I care more about what's going on with Safta. I'm going to Ella's tomorrow. Hopefully Tal will come over too. And hopefully I'll get a chance to see Shir separately, but I probably won't.

Abba drops Gili and me at Aunt Sigal's house. Gili

and the twins chase each other all over the small living room.

"You can't catch me! You can't catch me!" Gili teases them. In English.

The twins have a what-did-she-say look on their faces. The same one Gili used to have just six months ago when anyone spoke English to her.

"Hebrew," I say to her. It helps for a few minutes, and then she switches back to English.

"Girls," Aunt Sigal says, "please take the wild cousin chase outside." Within seconds they're in the backyard on the swing set.

"Shai." Aunt Sigal puts a hand on my shoulder. "Come on." I follow her to the far corner of her backyard. I know where we're going.

Her ceramic studio smells like clay, a nice change from the hospital smells.

"I have some pieces that I've made and already fired," Aunt Sigal says, pointing at a table with dozens of hearts. "Do you want to make Ema a new heart?"

Oh, she's heard the story of my stair surfing. "Sure!" I say. Good idea.

I used to like making my own pottery, but each piece takes a week to dry before you can put it in the kiln to harden. We'll be gone before I get a chance to add color.

Aunt Sigal hands me a heart, plus some brushes and paint. I stroke a dry brush on the heart. Staring at it.

Home is where the heart is. That's what the one I broke said. I'm not sure what that means anymore.

"I'm sorry I broke the one you made," I say to Aunt Sigal. "It was a special gift from you."

"You know what?" Aunt Sigal says. "I'll replicate the one you broke. That way it will still be my gift to my sister. You can make your own version."

"That sounds good," I say.

Aunt Sigal hands me an apron. She puts on her clay-smeared apron and sits next to me. I look down at the heart in front of me, still stroking it with the dry brush. I saw a magnet at a gift store in San Diego that said *Home is where Mom is.* It's not original, but neither is *Home is where the heart is.* That's what I'll write.

We work side by side in silence. When we're both done, Aunt Sigal puts the heart she made next to mine. "Your mom will love it," she says. Hers looks exactly like the one I broke.

I read them together.

Oh no. No. This is bad.

"Shai?" Aunt Sigal puts her hand on my shoulder. "Are you okay?"

I was thinking about myself when I wrote *Home is where Mom is,* but this is a gift for Ema. *Her* mom is here. And she'll leave her mom behind.

"I'll wrap these with bubble wrap once they're dry, so they won't break," Aunt Sigal says.

I want to break them. Both of them. But I can't say that to my aunt.

"Can I make another heart?" I ask Aunt Sigal.

"Of course you can." She sort of sings her answer.

I fill the heart with blue butterflies like I did on my cast.

"That's beautiful." Aunt Sigal is cheerfully singing again.

"I'm not done yet," I say. I'm planning to write on it once it's dry. "It's just the background."

"Want to make something for your dad too?" Aunt Sigal asks.

"Nah," I say.

"He looks a little worn out. It's probably hard for him. He surely didn't expect anything like this when he agreed to relocate."

I shrug.

"Are you still mad at him for moving?" she asks.

I nod. Kind of a circular nod, so Aunt Sigal can't figure out if it's a yes or a no. I'm not sure myself anymore.

"Looks like you girls have adjusted pretty well," she says.

She sees us now, but she has no idea how miserable we were before. Should I forgive Abba for putting his career before his family? For never asking us if we wanted to move halfway across the world? Was Jenny right to take the spot in art just because I like band now?

"He's a good man, your dad. I hope you know that." She puts her hand on my shoulder.

"But he cares more about non-browning avocados than he does about his family," I say.

"That's not true." Aunt Sigal takes off her apron. "It's not easy for him either, and this move wasn't all about the avocados. By taking this job, he gave you girls the chance to broaden your horizons, to perfect your English, to become citizens of the world. Not every kid gets such opportunities."

My eyes stay fixed on the new heart I made for Ema. Abba *is* a good man. She's right about that. I feel a lump the size of an avocado pit growing in my throat.

Aunt Sigal hangs up her clay-covered apron and hugs me tight. Her smell reminds me of Ema and Safta wrapped together in clay.

"I'll go call the girls," she says. "Maybe they'll want to paint hearts for Safta."

I take some white paint and mix just a tiny bit of yellow in it, so it will show better on the butterfly background. I touch the butterflies—dry enough. I use the thinnest brush Aunt Sigal has so it will all fit in.

The heart is big enough to have more than one place to call home.

I read it with my eyes, with my heart. I whisper it out loud. And I believe it.

CHAPTER 33

STOLEN BOYFRIEND, SHULA, AND SHOKO BANANA

I stand in front of Ella's house before I ring the doorbell. I stare at the carving on the fence. *Ella. Shai. Shir. Tal.* Hearts in between the names. At least our names are still together.

Ella's mom hugs me when I come in. It's like I never left. Ella shows me a picture of a new boy in school. Pretty cute, I have to admit.

"He was my boyfriend for a while," she says, "but then Shir stole him from me."

How can you steal a boy? It's not like he's a cell phone. I don't ask.

"Your friendship with Shir is more important than some cute boy," I say.

"Tell that to her," Ella says.

They'll have to sort it out themselves. I won't get to see Shir. I'm leaving tomorrow with Abba and Gili. My parents don't want us to miss too many school days. Ema is staying until the end of the week. I want to stay, and I want to go back, all at the same time.

I miss Kay-Lee. I guess this is how it's going to be now—I'll miss my friends in Israel when I'm in America and miss my friends in America when I'm in Israel. I always thought the feeling of missing someone belonged in the "sad emotions" category. But maybe it doesn't. If I had files of emotions-by-category in my head, I wouldn't know where to place it. To miss means to love—you only miss someone if you love them. Maybe having people you miss in your life belongs in a category all by itself. The happy-sad-lucky mixed-up category.

Tal comes over to Ella's house, and we all walk to the mini-market together to get ice cream bars. It's at the old part of the neighborhood where the houses are all one story and built close to each other. Everybody knows everybody, and everyone especially knows Shula, the owner of the mini-market.

"Shai!" Shula comes around from the counter to hug me. We used to come here every day after school.

"Shoko banana," Shula says. She remembers. "They don't have this in America, huh?" She hands me the chocolate-covered banana ice cream bar. "On the house. You two pay, though," she says to Ella and Tal. "Only the celebrity from America gets free ice cream today." Shula's belly bounces as she laughs.

She goes to the back office and comes back with a tray. "These aren't fresh, but they're still good. I made them yesterday. Take them. I bet you can't find bourekas in America either. Look how skinny you are. Nothing to eat there." Shula hands us three big bourekas. Much bigger than the ones Safta makes.

Ella takes out her wallet again. But Shula waves her money away like it's a fly. "The bourekas are my treat for the celebrity *and* her hosts."

"Thanks, Shula," Tal says as we leave. We cross the street and sit on a bench at the park. I miss this. Just walking everywhere, not needing Ema or Abba to drive me.

Shula's bourekas are almost as good as Safta's.

"There's really no bourekas in America?" Tal asks. "That sucks."

"There's something that looks like it but has apple filling," I say.

"How weird," Ella says.

Not weird, just different.

* * *

Abba, Gili, and I come to say goodbye to Safta before we leave. She's starting to look more like herself. Saba brought her favorite earrings—weirdly, the parrots match the hospital pajamas.

She's sitting up in bed, hugging the velvet diary. "Shai, binti." She gestures for me to sit on the bed next to her. "Thank you for bringing this. I gave it to your mom when she was your age. I wanted her to know I was once a teenager too. But as I revisited the young me in these pages, she reminded me so much of you. I want you to have it." She takes hold of my hand and spreads my fingers, as if she's about to read the future in my palm. I feel the weight of the diary as she places it in my hand, but it's lighter and softer without the guilt attached.

"Aunt Sigal is here!" Gili yells. "We have gifts for you, Safta."

The twins walk in slowly, carrying a box full of clay hearts. Gili grabs hers and waves it in Safta's face.

"I will hang it in the kitchen and think of you every time I see it," Safta says to Gili.

Aunt Sigal hands me a bag with my three hearts, all bubble-wrapped together. I'll give Ema the butterflies one and Aunt Sigal's new one in San Diego. I still want to throw away the *Home is where Mom is* one, but I don't want to undo the wrapping. I can get rid of it when we're back in America.

We all kiss and hug Safta—and Saba, who's back to his strangling hugs. Which is my final sign that things are going to be okay.

CHAPTER 34

JET LAG, BACKPACK, AND SPEAKING UP

We got home late last night, but still I wake up before sunrise. Jet lag's fault again. I pull Safta's diary from the bottom of my suitcase. Maybe I should've asked Safta for permission to have Faiza translate the parts written in Arabic to English, but actually I should let Safta do it, so the whole diary will be in Hebrew. And maybe one day I'll translate it all to English.

I make lunch sandwiches for school for Gili and me, just the way Ema does. Then I make another one. For Abba.

The doorbell rings, and before I wipe my hands, Gili flies down the stairs, getting to the door first and opening it wide. Motek jumps on her. Abba and I come to the door at the same time.

Motek goes back and forth from one person to another, like he's not sure who he missed most. Or he's collecting evidence to figure out where we've been.

"Come in," Abba says to Kay-Lee, who is standing

in her polka-dot pajamas with a plate of snickerdoodles in her hands.

"OMG, sneaker-poodles," I say. Kay-Lee and I both laugh. Abba has no clue why, but he smiles all the same. I set the cookies on the counter and give her a hug.

"I have to go get dressed," she says. "See you at school."

* * *

I doze through most of the morning classes until the bell for lunch finally wakes me up. I scan the lunch area for extra color.

Hands cover my eyes from behind—hands that smell like snickerdoodles.

I turn around. Blue jeans, black-and-white checkered shirt. "Kay-Lee?"

She hugs me. "Don't look so surprised. I'm just making up for lost time. I've been banning two important colors for too long."

"Hi," a soft voice behind us says. "Can I sit with you?"

We both turn around. It's Olivia.

"I'm so sorry, Shai," she says. "I never thought you stole my phone. I never meant to hurt you. You are the nicest person I ever met. Madison, Mia, and Mikaela were my only friends since kindergarten, and I was afraid they might replace me with Jenny. But that's no excuse."

She looks at Kay-Lee. "I've always secretly loved that you have the guts to wear whatever you feel like wearing. I'm sorry I never had the guts to say it out loud." She's squeezing her elbows with her opposite hands the whole time she's talking. "Sorry." She looks back and forth at both of us.

"I forgive you," I say. I forgave her a long time ago.

Kay-Lee scoots over to make room for Olivia between us.

"Did you hear about Pat and Hakim?" Olivia asks.

I shake my head no.

"I just heard," Kay-Lee says. "Hakim got expelled."

I can't believe this.

"He only got suspended," Olivia says. "Pat was expelled. From what I've heard, Hakim beat Pat up pretty bad."

"That doesn't sound like Hakim," I say.

The bell rings before I get to hear the rest of the story.

"See you in PE," Olivia says.

* * *

"What happened with Pat and Hakim?" I ask Chris as soon as I see him in PE.

"Welcome back," he says.

"Thanks. So what happened?"

"Pat followed Hakim after school and pushed him to the ground at the park right across the street. He pulled off Hakim's backpack, saying there was a bomb in it. Then he threw the backpack into the fountain."

"Oh no."

"That's when Hakim punched him in the face."

I bring my hand to my face, feeling like I'm the one who's just been punched.

"It was off school grounds but right after school, so Pat's parents got the school involved."

"But Pat started it," I say. Heat rushes to my ears.

"Yeah, but Hakim was the one who got physically violent."

"After Pat pushed him! This is so unfair!"

And it's my fault.

I should've spoken up about the yellow Star of David. I'm such a sausage. If I had reported Pat then, he would've been expelled a long time ago. I could've spared Hakim from this bullying.

"He'll be back in school next week," Chris says in a voice much less confident than his fact-stating one. "It's not that bad, Shai."

"It is," I say. I have to talk to Hakim.

* * *

After school, I go straight to Hakim's.

My body thinks it's nighttime and my stomach is twisted. Not sure I can blame jet lag for all of it.

Faiza opens the door when I knock. "Shai, binti!" She hugs me. It's always going to make my heart wobbly when she calls me that. "How is your grandma doing?" she asks.

I tell her that Safta was released from the hospital a few days ago. She hugs me again.

"Hakim!" Faiza hollers. "Visitor."

Hakim comes down the stairs. His hair is all messed up, like he's been lying in bed in the same position for too long. "Hey." He sounds half awake. "You're back."

I move my hand in a short, slow-motion wave. "Can we talk?"

"Sure," Hakim says, running a hand through his messy hair. "Let's sit in the backyard."

"I'll bring some tea and baklava," Faiza says, more to me then to Hakim.

"She's been upset with me since I got suspended," Hakim says as she rushes to the kitchen, "but she can never resist the urge to feed anyone who walks through the door."

Sounds like Safta. I smile.

Their backyard is beautiful—so many flowers blooming it's hard to believe it's winter.

"I'm sorry about Pat," I say.

"It's not your fault Pat's a jerk."

But it is my fault his jerkiness wasn't revealed earlier.

"Baklava." Faiza shows up with a full tray of treats and her fancy teacups. She sets it all on the table and leaves.

"You were right," I say. "I should've gone straight to the principal when Pat gave me the Star of David." I stare at the flowers on the teacup.

Hakim doesn't say anything. He doesn't have to.

I know that I can still speak up. I owe it to Hakim. I owe it to anyone who might ever get bullied by Pat— or by anyone like him.

We eat baklava. We both pull out the pistachios.

Faiza comes by with another plate. "What's wrong with you two?" She slaps her leg. "The pistachios are the best part."

Hakim and I look at the plate of dates she just set in front of us and laugh.

CHAPTER 35
THREE HEARTS, HUGS, AND EMA

From down the street, I see Abba at the door, like a door-man waiting to take my coat. I should tell him about Pat right now. No, I'll wait for the weekend when Ema comes back. I'll tell them together.

He's waving something in his hand.

"This came in the mail for you when we were gone," he says and hands me a blue-and-green envelope.

Children for Peace. How is that possible? I never entered the competition.

I open the envelope slowly. *We are pleased to inform you that the drawing you submitted for the Children for Peace competition has been selected as one of the top ten finalists . . .* What? How?

The only person who knew about this was Kay-Lee.

"What is it?" Abba asks. "Where are you going?"

"To Kay-Lee's," I yell and run out the door.

* * *

"Read this." I wave the letter in Kay-Lee's face.

She does. Then she hugs me and starts jumping up and down. Then she stops. "Are you mad?"

I smile.

"I kind of wandered up to your room when I was watching Motek, and I found the drawing. I figured you forgot to send it with everything going on. So I sent it in for you. I looked on their website and followed the directions for scanning. I almost missed the deadline."

"I've never had a friend like you," I say.

She flops on her bed and pushes a pile of clothes to the floor. I sit next to her.

"I talked to my mom," she says.

"That's great!" Oh, oops—maybe not. But she's smiling. It *is* great.

"She's been getting treatment. She feels better and hopes we give her a second chance to be our mom. She wants us to visit her in France." Kay-Lee strokes her quilt. "But she doesn't have the money to get us tickets. And my dad sure doesn't either. Besides the bakery, he's spending lots of money on doctors to try to help Zoe start talking again."

Couldn't he sell the bakery? I don't dare say it out loud.

"My grandma keeps trying to convince him to sell the bakery," Kay-Lee says, as if reading my mind. "But he says he has to make it profitable first. I think he doesn't want to sell it because he still hopes my mom will come back." She sighs. "I wish we could afford to visit her."

I'll win the round-trip ticket. I'll choose a round trip to France, which I'll give to Kay-Lee. "I have a good feeling about this," I say. "You'll go soon."

Kay-Lee just looks at me. Serious for a second, and then she smiles. "Do you still want to do a mural at the bakery? That might bring people in."

"Let's do it!" I say.

"Can we do it this weekend?" Kay-Lee asks. "My dad says early Saturday morning would be the best time."

"Sure," I say, even though I hoped to go with Abba to pick up Ema from the airport. "We can do a colorful version of the Eiffel Tower if you want."

"That would be awesome," she says. "I have to tell my mom about it. I can send her pictures." Kay-Lee looks like all the colors of her clothing are flowing in her heart.

"Don't forget this." She hands me my peace drawing. It's better than I remembered.

When I get home, Abba and Gili are making a cake for Ema. I lay my drawing on the only clean spot on the kitchen counter.

"Wow!" Abba says. "This is amazing, Shai."

"Let me see." Gili jumps up and down.

"Be careful not to get flour on Shai's masterpiece," Abba says.

I've never seen him so excited about my art. "Can I have it?" he asks. "I'd love to give it to our advertising department, if you agree. It would be perfect for a brochure we're working on."

I laugh. "This is supposed to represent world peace."

"Well, look again," Abba says. "It looks like feeding the world to me."

It reminds me of something my art teacher at the museum used to say: Art can be interpreted by the viewer in ways that the artist didn't intend. This is probably what she meant.

"What does that have to do with non-browning avocados?" I ask.

Abba's eyes light up like fireflies, flickering behind his glasses. "I'm so glad you asked! With our technology, we increase productivity and decrease waste."

"But . . ." I don't want to argue with him, but I have to. "Isn't it also risky? What about long-term effects?" I stare at the floor to avoid Abba's look, but he lifts my chin. He's smiling a big, proud smile.

"I'm glad you're asking questions, Shai. You're asking the right questions. Always ask. There have been thousands of studies over the past thirty years, done by multiple agencies. These foods are safe."

I look down at the floor again. "It still feels wrong to eat something that isn't natural."

Abba sighs. "Think of it this way. In less than a hundred years, the world population has grown from two billion to over seven billion. We have to try new things in order to keep feeding the growing population of the world. With genetic engineering, we use less water, less land, and less fertilizer, all while producing less waste."

I don't know what to believe anymore. "What if your company is sponsored by a big organization that just wants to make money?" I dare to lift my gaze, and our eyes meet.

Abba sighs. "It's true that greed can lead to harmful use of GMO technology. Unfortunately, greed sometimes causes more harm than good in other industries too. But my lab isn't sponsored by any corporation, and if my goal in life was to make money, I wouldn't have become a scientist."

I try to smile. I want to trust my dad.

"So what do you say? Can I use your drawing?" Abba asks.

"Okay," I say. Because even though I'm not sure I'm pro-GMO, I know I'm pro-Abba.

"I'm proud of you," he says, holding my drawing in his hand.

"I'm sorry I gave you a hard time about moving," I blurt out.

"I know," he says and kisses the top of my head.

I go upstairs and unpack the ceramic hearts from the bubble wrap. All three survived the trip to San Diego.

Home is where Mom is can stay tucked in the bottom of my sock drawer. Shifting socks to the side to make room for it, I feel the coolness of a thin metal string. My necklace.

I forgot how pretty it is. I forgot how much I love it. I stand in front of the mirror and put it back on. Not because Saba supports it, not because Pat's been expelled, but because this is who I am—who I'm proud to be.

I take the other two ceramic hearts downstairs.

"Where are the nails?" I ask Abba. He's covered in flour. So is Gili.

I show him the two hearts.

"The heart is big enough to have more than one place to call home." He reads it out loud. He stands still for a minute, staring at the heart.

"You know I love you?" he says and gives me a floury hug.

I know. But it's nice to hear.

Abba brings me the nails and Ema's sparkly hammer. I hang Aunt Sigal's new heart where the original was and put mine right next to it.

"Ema will love it," Abba says.

I don't think she'll love the way the kitchen looks.

In the morning, Abba tries to make French toast, creating an even bigger mess. He's whistling and dancing as he's flipping them. The French toast actually smells like Ema's, but the slices look pretty smooshed and extremely unappetizing. I go to Kay-Lee's, skipping breakfast.

Mr. Park drives us to the bakery. He's opening earlier than usual, so we can get a head start on the mural before customers come in.

I've printed a detailed sketch of the Eiffel Tower. First, I trace all the Eiffel's lines onto the wall. And it's a whole lot of lines. You don't really realize what an image is made of until you copy it. I now appreciate the Eiffel Tower more.

"That looks awesome," Kay-Lee says when I'm done.

The smell of fresh croissants floods my nostrils. "Time for some color!" I announce.

Kay-Lee brings about ten cans of paint. "Can I help?" she asks.

"Sure." I wave a paintbrush her way like a wand. "Let's make some magic."

When we're done, it looks like a rainbow exploded inside the bakery. The rest of the walls in black and white complement the colorful Eiffel perfectly.

Mr. Park stares at our work with sparkly eyes. "I love it," he says. "Thank you, Shai. Croissants on the house for the two artists." He claps his hands.

I look at the black-and-white clock on the wall. "I should be heading home soon. My mom will be back in an hour."

"Can you drop us at home, Dad?" Kay-Lee asks. "I have something for Shai."

Mr. Park packs two more croissants to go and grabs the car keys.

Safta-Harmony and Zoe are out on the Parks' front porch reading the turtle book.

"Zoe," Kay-Lee says, "guess who's coming back from Israel today?"

Zoe looks at me and smiles.

"She loves your ema," Kay-Lee says.

"Mural all done?" Safta-Harmony asks.

"You *have* to see it," Kay-Lee says. "It's super amazing."

Zoe pulls on Safta-Harmony's sleeve.

"We can go later. Now Shai has to try on her dress."

"Heyyyyy, it's supposed to be a surprise!" Kay-Lee says.

"Surprise time is now!" Safta-Harmony waves her hands in the air.

Kay-Lee runs upstairs and comes down holding a bright blue dress.

My hand goes to my mouth, then moves to my heart. The dress is patterned like butterfly wings.

"Try it on." Kay-Lee hands it to me.

The fabric is smooth and cool. "It's beautiful," I manage to say.

I go to the bathroom and slip out of my shorts and T-shirt, like a butterfly making its way out of a cocoon. It's a perfect fit.

I never imagined myself in a dress like this. It's so not me, but at the same time, maybe it is. Maybe this is what a butterfly feels like the first minute it turns into one.

When I come out of the bathroom, Safta-Harmony claps and says, "Beautiful!"

I hug Kay-Lee.

Zoe pulls on my dress and points out the window.

"They're here," I tell Kay-Lee.

Zoe runs outside. Kay-Lee and I follow.

"Ema is here!" Gili shouts through the car's window.

"Ema!" Zoe cries.

Kay-Lee grabs my arm.

I want to go hug Ema, but I let Zoe beat me to it, and I hug Kay-Lee instead.

"She talked. Zoe talked." Kay-Lee looks like she's about to cry. She runs to hug Zoe.

I go hug Ema. "Look at that beautiful dress," she says, and when she squeezes me tight, I feel home is where my mom is.

We all go into the house. Abba puts down Ema's

suitcase and points to the wall. Ema's gaze follows his finger and lands on the two ceramic hearts.

"Shai," she whispers. "Wow! I love them. I love you."

She hugs me tight again. I melt into her hug and think about the third heart I left in my sock drawer—*Home is where Mom is.*

Maybe one day I'll give it to Kay-Lee.

CHAPTER 36

A BiG DISAPPOINTMENT AND A GENIUS iDEA

I recognize the blue-and-green Children for Peace envelope when Gili brings in the mail.

I snatch it out of Gili's hands, and I give it to Ema. "Open it for me," I say. I want her to be proud.

She opens it carefully, like she's going to reuse the envelope. Come on already! She reads silently. "I'm so proud of you," she says.

I knew it!

"Honorable mention is such an achievement," she says.

Wait, what?

I take the letter from her hand. Honorable mention? Who needs this honor? I need to help Kay-Lee get to France. I flop onto the sofa in the living room. I crinkle the letter into a ball and throw it across the room.

"What is the matter with you?" Ema stands by the sofa with her hands on her hips.

Motek runs to the honorable-mention ball and brings it back to me. Tears well up in my eyes.

Ema sits next to me and puts her arm around my shoulder. "You should be proud of yourself for getting an honorable mention."

"But . . . I was planning to . . ." I try to explain that I needed to win the first prize, that I needed the plane ticket to help Kay-Lee.

Abba bursts into the house. "The marketing team loves Shai's drawing! It's going to be on the front cover of our brochure."

"That's great," Ema says, "and look what just came in the mail!" She walks toward him, waving the not-so-honorable wrinkled letter. "It won an honorable mention in the competition."

"Wow, congratulations!" Abba says before he spots me slouched on the living room couch. "Shai?" He walks toward me. "Why the long face? We should celebrate this."

Ema's right behind him. They're both standing above me with the same why-aren't-you-happy expression on their faces.

"You don't understand. I needed to win the prize . . ."

"Needed?" Abba asks.

"It shouldn't be about the prize," Ema says.

"It was. I wanted the plane ticket." I try to explain. I don't want them to think I'm ungrateful. "First, I wanted it for myself, to go to Israel. But then I wanted it for Kay-Lee, so she can go visit her mom in France."

"Oh, Shai." Ema sits next to me, collecting me into her arms. Tucked in the warmth of her hug, I melt into her. She absorbs my disappointment.

Abba situates himself on the edge of the ottoman right in front of me. "Kay-Lee is lucky to have you as a friend."

I look from Abba to Ema. "There's something else I need to tell you."

"You can tell us anything. Always," Ema says. She gathers all my hair to the back, like she would if I was about to throw up, like she knows I *am* about to throw up—ugly words that I couldn't digest.

The words gush from my mouth like vomit, rushed and garbled until it's all out. The whole story of Pat and the yellow Star of David.

Abba pops up like he's been bitten by a snake. But after a second, he sits back down. He slides his glasses up on top of his head and presses his fingers to his eyes like he's trying to squeeze something out of them.

A storm roars in my stomach. Why isn't he saying anything?

Ema's hand moves from my hair to my knee. Tears float in her big blue eyes.

Abba gets up again, this time slowly. His eyes are red from the squeeze he gave them.

"I'm . . . I . . ." Words are finally coming out of his mouth, but the voice isn't his. It's the voice of someone lost. My abba is never lost.

Finally, he explodes. "The school should be notified. There should be consequences. Who is this guy? Who are his parents?" His lost voice is eaten up by an unrecognizable, monstrous voice.

"He just got expelled," I say. "He got into a fight with my friend Hakim. He called him a terrorist."

Abba walks to the dining room table and bangs a fist on it. "Motek!" he calls out. Motek rushes over to him. "I'm taking the dog for a walk," he mumbles.

"Now, Oren? Really?" Ema asks. "You can't run away from this. We need to talk."

"I'm not running away," Abba says. "I need to think. We'll talk when I get back."

"This is very serious, Shai," Ema says.

The storm in my stomach surges through the rest of my body. "I know." My voice is barely a whisper.

"Some people in this world carry despicable beliefs," Ema says. "Never be silent when facing them, Shai." She sighs and gathers me into a hug. "I'm sorry you had to experience that."

"You're strangling me," I choke, and Ema loosens her hug, still gripping me at arm's length.

Her gaze falls on my necklace. "You put it back on." She half-smiles. "Good for you."

I touch the star on my neck, shifting it from side to side.

"You haven't been wearing it for a long while," Ema says. She's holding on to her own arms now, like she's hugging herself. "I'm sorry I never asked why you took it off."

"I'm sorry I didn't tell you."

"We'll figure this out," she says. I put my head on her lap, and she strokes my hair just like she used to do when I was little and couldn't fall asleep.

I hear Motek's footsteps and collar clinking, beating Abba into the living room. They're back already. I sit up. Abba's silence vibrates through the house, stirring up the storm in my stomach again.

He lowers himself to the couch. "I'm sorry, Shai. I was too wrapped up in contributing to scientific progress. But there's still antisemitism in this world, and I've exposed you all to it. Maybe I shouldn't have taken the job here."

"Oren . . ." Ema says softly.

Abba looks at her. "We should have at least sent the girls to a private Jewish school, like your dad suggested."

"What you're doing is important and being here is important. Hiding from antisemitism isn't going to make it disappear," Ema says.

I sit up straight. "I never would've met Hakim if we didn't move here. Or if we went to a Jewish school," I say. "Abba, you fix genes to keep fruit from rotting and help feed the world. Hakim and I should stick together against rotten people to help fix the world."

Abba takes a deep breath, like he's aiming to let all the air in the room into his lungs. He looks at me like he's trying to figure out who I am. "I'm so proud of you, Shai. Maybe Hakim's parents would want to join us in filing a complaint. It's a serious matter," he says. He looks older than he is. "I hope you understand how serious this is."

I nod.

"But I'm proud that you're approaching it with a positive and mature attitude. Let's sleep on it and decide."

I hug him. I hug him like I mean it—because I do.

"Thank you," he whispers into my hair, and I wish I gave him this hug a long time ago.

"How about bourekas for dinner?" Ema asks. "To celebrate Shai's honorable mention."

I almost forgot about that. I roll my eyes.

"Shai, you can invite Kay-Lee over for dinner," Ema says.

Kay-Lee. Bourekas. The bakery. Why didn't I think of it before? "Yes, bourekas!" I yell, and I sprint to Kay-Lee's house.

Kay-Lee opens the door. I'm panting and talking at the same time. "How about we make bourekas?"

What? She doesn't say it. I'm just really good at reading facial expressions.

"For the bakery," I say, catching my breath. "Safta's bourekas. I bet they would be a hit. There's nothing like it here."

"You're a genius," Kay-Lee says.

* * *

I make a big sign that says *Safta's pastries. Pay for ten, get a dozen.* We hang it in the front window of the bakery.

Mr. Park has bought all the ingredients. Safta-Harmony, with a white apron and a huge smile, helps Gili and Zoe up onto stools. She cuts the dough into squares, just like Ema taught her, and the girls put the filling in the center and fold them into triangles. I pinch the edges and brush them with egg. Kay-Lee spreads sesame seeds on them. The smell of the bourekas fills the bakery.

Chris and Hakim come by. Mr. Park comes out of the kitchen and gives them bourekas. "On the house," he says. Feels almost like I'm back in Israel at Shula's mini-market. I wish Mr. Park had shoko banana ice cream bars. That really would be a bestseller.

"Did you know that the origin of bourekas is actually Turkey?" Chris says. "Also, Bulgaria and a few more countries had them before they became traditional in Israel. In fact, any of the Balkan countries—"

Hakim elbows him. "Okay, geek, whatever. Just eat."

I pull Hakim to the side and tell him I'm going with my parents to talk to the principal tomorrow morning.

He swallows the last bite of the bourekas in his hand and nods. There's a shimmer in his eyes that tells me I'm doing the right thing. "We make a good team, you and I," he says. Crumbs of flaky bourekas fall on his sweatshirt. I point at them. He laughs, shaking them off.

"We do make a good team," I say. Wishing for a world where everyone is on the same team—team humans.

A customer walks in. "What's that wonderful smell?"

Mr. Park smiles at me and gives the lady a sample.

"See?" I tell Kay-Lee. "It's going to be a hit. I see Paris in your near future. Who knows—you might even end up living in France one day."

"No way," Kay-Lee says.

"Why not? A new world, a new language, a new culture. Could be exciting." I can't believe I'm saying this. I can't believe I'm believing it as I say it.

"You think so?" she asks.

"I do." I really do. "One thing is for sure. You're going to Paris this summer."

"I'm starting to believe that maybe I am," she says.

"Focus on the good," I say. "Focus on the good."

ACKNOWLEDGMENTS

I wish there was room on the front cover for the names of those I list here on the last page.

Without their help from the very beginning, I would have never reached THE END.

The Society of Children's Book Writers and Illustrators (SCBWI) was my starting point, and it's where I found answers, resources, wonderful like-minded people, and the most fabulous and supportive critique group I could have hoped for. Thank you to Cindy Schuricht, Scott Gallear, Linda Kao, Lauri Patton, and Kris Guy for helping me raise Shai to be the published teenager she is today. (Linda, thanks for the title too!)

I am thankful to my kindhearted and talented writing friends: Sally Pla, Colleen Paeff, and Laurel Hendrix, whose support and insights have made this book much better.

Thank you, Tina Burke (my first non-writer friend to read the first full draft), Nami Boaz, Maya Cohen, and many more, near and far, for encouraging and supporting me throughout the years and tears it took to write this book—you know who you are and I love you all.

How lucky am I to have been mentored by the thoughtful and generous (and Newbery Award-winning!) Tae Keller. Thank you and the entire team behind AuthorMentorMatch—I would most likely still be in the querying trenches without you.

To my wise and trustworthy agent, Melissa Edwards of Stonesong Literary Agency, who believed in the importance and relevance of Shai's story. To Joni Sussman, who welcomed Shai into the Kar-Ben family warmheartedly, and to the rest of the Kar-Ben and Lerner team.

To Catriella Freedman and the PJ Our Way committee for granting me the Author Incentive Award.

To my own one-of-a-kind ema, Liora Lichtenberg, who cried and laughed in all the right places in every draft she read, and to my abba, Dov Lichtenberg, for passing on to me his passion for writing and for relentlessly asking me when was I going to finish writing this book already. (I did it, Abba.)

To my three wonders, Guy, Shai, and Adi—being your mom inspires everything I do. This book is greatly inspired by all of you (yeah, Guy, you too!).

To my husband, Nir Nimrodi, whose involvement with the development of the non-browning Arctic apple inspired my non-browning avocados—thanks for being my source for all things GMO, but mostly for being my anchor, my biggest believer, my constant cheerleader, my everything. This book would have remained just an idea in my head without your faith in me.

Last, but not least, I thank you, dear reader, for sticking around for Shai's story. There are so many wonderful books out there and I know you can never read them all—I'm grateful to you for choosing to read mine.

Thank you for focusing on the good while peacefully battling the bad to make our world a better place. Wherever your home may be, I hope you're surrounded with love.

ABOUT THE AUTHOR

Noa has been drawing faces without noses since early childhood—in Israel, in the United States, and on airplanes back and forth. As a designer, Noa worked on displays in bookshops and gravitated most to children's books, sparking her passion to create her own. Two of her Hebrew-language picture books, one which she also illustrated, have been published in Israel.

Noa lives near the ocean in Southern California with her husband and two dogs. She travels around the world, often to visit her three grown children, who all call more than one place home.